HONOR OF THE WITCH

WITCHES OF KEATING HOLLOW, BOOK 12

DEANNA CHASE

Copyright © 2022 by Deanna Chase

Editing: Angie Ramey

Cover image: © Ravven

ISBN 978-1-953422-45-3

Bayou Moon Press, LLC

www.deannachase.com

Printed in the United States of America

ABOUT THIS BOOK

There's a reason Brinn Taylor will never leave Keating Hollow. It's the only town that gives her peace from ghosts who haunt her. As an adult, Brinn has everything she's ever wanted. Well, almost everything. The one person she'd had to give up was Austin Steele, the love of her life, when he left town to follow his own dreams. Only now he's back, and he's bidding on her at the first annual bachelorette auction. The problem? He's only in town temporarily, and getting close to him again isn't an option.

The moment Austin Steele drives into Keating Hollow, all he wants to do is reconnect with Brinn Taylor. Unfortunately, she's not interested. And for good reason. Once he settles his grandmother's estate, he's headed back out of town to the life he's built for himself. But when there's a mystery to solve regarding his grandmother's estate, there's only one person who can help him—Brinn Taylor. Now he's ready to do whatever it takes to get back into her good graces... even if it means bidding a fortune for her company at a charity auction.

CHAPTER 1

*B*rinn Taylor made her way to the counter of Witches in Stitches, Keating Hollow's newest yarn store, and stared at her cousin's stash of skeins in disbelief. "You're buying all of that today?"

"Of course I am," Wanda said and grinned at her. "If something's worth doing, it's worth overdoing. Right, Blake?"

Blake, Wanda's half sister, brushed her long dark hair off her shoulder and rolled her eyes at Wanda. "Your craft room is already overflowing with projects. You're going to have to have Cam build you a she-shed if you keep this up."

Wanda sniffed and straightened her shoulders. "It's not a craft room. It's a studio, and there's plenty of space if I just buy some more rolling organizers."

Brinn laughed as she shook her head. The two women couldn't be more different. Wanda had fiery red hair and the personality to match. Blake had dark hair and dark eyes and was far quieter than her larger-than-life sister. It wasn't that Blake was shy, she just tended to take longer to open up to those around her.

"Is that all *you're buying*?" Wanda asked Brinn, raising one eyebrow.

"I only need one skein to get started," Brinn insisted. She turned to the older woman standing next to her. "Right, Ms. Betty?"

"That's right, dear," Ms. Betty said, her white hair bobbing as she nodded enthusiastically. "Crocheting is just like dating. One is good when you're starting out, but once you have some experience, you're going to want to try them all." She gave Brinn an exaggerated wink. "That's how I found out I like my yarn just like my men—super bulky."

Brinn let out a cackle. "Where do you find these super bulky men?"

"The gym over at Enchanted Dreams," she said with a shrug, referring to the retirement village on the outskirts of Keating Hollow. "They don't have anything else to do besides pump iron and meet for happy hour."

"You're saying the men over at your retirement village have six-pack abs?" Brinn asked, highly amused by the older woman.

"More like six packs of empty beer cans," Betty said with a snort. "Though Xavier has the forearms of a fifty-year-old." She curled her hand into a claw shape and added, "Raaarh. That man gets me going just by rolling up his shirtsleeves."

Brinn smiled at her. "I want to be you when I grow up."

"Oh, sweetheart. Don't wait forty years to start," Ms. Betty said, patting Brinn's arm. "Go out and find yourself a man... or woman," she added with a wink, "with a set of forearms that revs your engine and get it, girl."

"If only." Brinn let out a sigh. "It seems I'm always attracted to ones who can't wait to leave Keating Hollow."

"They don't all leave, Brinn," Wanda said, side-eyeing her cousin. "You know that."

Brinn shrugged. It was true. Plenty of good men stayed. But the only one Brinn had ever loved had left and never looked back five years ago. He'd disappeared, leaving only a letter. No forwarding address. No phone number. No calls. And she'd been heartbroken. Dating after that had just been a chore. "If only I'd fallen for one of them."

"Brinn," Ms. Betty said. "You don't need to fall for a guy to enjoy his forearms." She waggled her eyebrows, a mischievous gleam in her eyes. "How do you think I stay so young? It's not all that cold cream the beauty industry tries to push on us *mature* women."

Chuckling, Brinn paid for her yarn and said, "Whatever you're doing, it's working for you."

"You should let it work for you, too," Ms. Betty insisted. "It will do wonders for your complexion."

Wanda threw her head back and cackled as they watched the older woman cross the shop to the classroom where they were all gathering in a few minutes. "You should listen to her, Brinn. It's been far too long since you've been out on a date and even longer since you had... any forearms to rev your engine."

"Stop," Brinn insisted, waving a dismissive hand. "I don't need a reminder about my pathetic love life."

"Oh, no. I'm sorry," Wanda said, giving her a sympathetic frown. "You know I didn't mean it like that, right?"

"Sure," Brinn said, forcing a smile. The fact was, she did know that her cousin wasn't trying to make her feel bad. All she wanted was for Brinn to have some fun.

"I don't think you do," Wanda said, suddenly sounding fierce. She took Brinn's hands in both of hers and squeezed them as she stared her in the eyes. "No one thinks you need a man to make you whole. No one, and especially not me." She let out a bark of laughter. "Remember when I used to say I was too set in my ways to live with a man?"

Brinn couldn't help it. She smiled and nodded. "Yep. No one was more surprised than me when you hooked up with Cameron."

"Except me." Wanda grinned. "Here's the thing. I was happy before he came along. And if he hadn't, I'd still be that same happy person. But sharing my life with him is something special too. All I'm saying here is that I don't want you to close yourself off to possibilities. I want you to have fun and enjoy yourself. You're young; enjoy it. Try not to take it so seriously."

She meant dating. Brinn understood what her cousin was trying to say. Ever since Austin had broken Brinn's heart, she'd pretty much sworn off dating and men altogether. The idea of losing someone she loved again… It was just too much. But a date certainly didn't need to lead to anything serious, did it? She knew lots of women her age who dated casually. Why couldn't she do the same?

Brinn nodded slowly. "Yeah, I think you're right. Maybe I should get out there again."

"I'll help you set up a dating app profile," Blake said, already pulling out her phone.

Wanda turned to her sister with a curious expression. "What do you know about dating apps? Do you have a profile out there?"

"What if I did?" Blake raised a questioning eyebrow. "Is that a problem?"

"No, I just…" Wanda let out a frustrated huff. "I know you're not a child, but if you're going to be meeting strangers off the internet, we should really set up some safety protocols just to keep you safe."

Blake smirked. "Like what? Having you call ten minutes into the date with an emergency? Or were you thinking something a little more hands on, like eating at the same restaurant so that you can follow us after we leave? I could always just hire you as my driver. Then I'd always have an escort, just like the olden days."

"Okay, smartass," Wanda said with her hands on her hips. "Seriously? Have you been meeting strange men off the internet?"

Blake rolled her eyes. "No, *Mom*. But I did consider it. It's not like Keating Hollow is overflowing with boys my age."

"There's Cam," Wanda pointed out, referring to Cameron's son.

"Cam and I are... friends," Blake said, shifting her gaze so she wasn't meeting her sister's eyes.

"I see." Wanda slipped her arm through Blake's and started to lead her over to the couches. "Just promise me you'll let me know if you meet someone from a hookup app or go on any sort of blind date."

"Will you follow me with your golf cart?" Blake mused.

"Probably." Wanda turned her attention to Brinn as the three of them took their seats across from Ms. Betty. Miss Maple, the owner of the shop a few doors down, A Spoon Full of Magic, sat next to her with her crochet hook already moving quickly through a ball of yarn. "I'll follow Brinn, too. No one goes on a date with an internet stranger without a backup plan. Got it?"

"Who said I'm going out on a date with an internet stranger?" Brinn asked. She was not at all excited about hookup apps. She was more the type to meet someone in person and then decide if there was any chemistry. That was also probably why she hadn't been on a date in forever. Besides the bookstore, where was she going to meet anyone?

"Oh, sweetie. Have you tried Winker yet?" Ms. Betty asked.

"Winker?" Brinn frowned. "What's that?"

"You know, that dating app where you wink at the hotties and if they wink back, you're a match." Ms. Betty pulled out her phone and brought up her profile. "Oh, hot damn. Look at this one." She flipped the phone around, revealing a tall, heavily tanned man with white hair. "Isn't he just lickable?"

"With all that hair coming out of his ears?" Blake asked. "I think he could use a day at the spa first."

"Pshaw!" Ms. Betty shook her head. "He can be trained. Men will do just about anything to get a piece of this." She waved a hand, indicating her body, and gave them a Cheshire Cat grin. "One word from me and he'd have that ear hair trimmer out faster than you can say hairy beast."

"Okay. Well anyway..." Brin stared down at her ball of yarn and wondered when the class was going to start.

"We should sign Brinn up for the bachelorette auction," Miss Maple said.

"That is a fantastic idea," Wanda said, her tone full of excitement. "I can't believe I didn't think about that. It's low pressure, a bunch of us will be there, and it raises money for the Artist in Residence program the town council is putting together."

"You're going to be in a bachelorette auction?" Brinn asked her cousin. "What does Cam think of that?"

Wanda waved a dismissive hand. "It's just for fun and charity. It's not like I'm going to actually date the winner. It's just an afternoon of my time. No big deal. But you on the other hand, you just might find the man of your dreams."

"I don't think—" Brinn started, not liking where this was going. The idea of auctioning herself off for a date seemed rather desperate.

"Oh, come on, Brinn. Blake is going to do it," Wanda said.

"I am?" Blake asked, looking surprised.

"Yes." Wanda gave her a pointed look. "I asked you about it last week. Remember? I said you could make your date shortbread cookies?"

"Right," Blake said with a nod. "It's coming back to me now. You said you'd loan me your golf cart if I offered myself up, and then added I should make a double batch of shortbread so that you'd get some. I'm pretty sure I only told you'd I'd think about it."

Wanda chuckled. "Sounds about right. But I signed you up already. You don't want to disappoint Miss Maple, do you?"

Blake raised a skeptical eyebrow and then glanced at Miss Maple. "Would you really be disappointed?"

The owner of the A Spoon Full of Magic shook her head. "No, dear. But we would really appreciate if you could help us out. There's just not that many single gals here in Keating Hollow anymore, and none as young and pretty as you."

"How am I supposed to say no to that?" Blake asked Brinn, clearly looking for help.

"I have no idea," Brinn said, unable to keep from chuckling. "These ladies are just impossible to turn down."

"Excellent," Miss Maple said, rubbing her hands together. "Then you'll both participate?"

Blake threw her head back and laughed. When she contained herself, she smirked at Brinn. "You had your chance to get out of this and blew it."

"You're right. I did." Brinn turned to Miss Maple and said,

"I hope you find some cute guys to bid on us, because I'm not dealing with ear hair."

"Don't you worry, ladies. We've got that covered," Ms. Betty insisted.

Brinn had her doubts, but there was really no way to bow out gracefully. At least Blake would be there. It couldn't be that bad, could it? "What kind of date are we committing to? A picnic or something like that?"

"Anything you want. The only stipulation is that it happens right after the auction," Miss Maple said. "A few hours of your time is all you have to commit to."

Brinn frowned. "Normally I'd go for a date to the coast or a hike in the woods, but considering it's been forty degrees out all month, I'll probably have to come up with something else."

"You should just Netflix and chill," Ms. Betty said.

"Ms. Betty!" Brinn choked out a laugh. "Do you even know what that means?"

"Of course I do." The older woman made a face, indicating that she was offended. "I'm hip."

Wanda snickered. "I'm not sure that's the word the kids use these days for being in the know."

Ms. Betty grabbed her crochet hook and started working on her foundation chain. "So maybe I'm not up on all my slang, but I do know that inviting a hottie over to Netflix and chill takes all the guesswork out of it. You both know the expectation. If he's any good and you like him, then you can ask him out for a real date."

"So you're basically test-driving him first?" Brinn asked.

"Of course. At my age, I don't really have time to waste." She winked at them.

Everyone laughed and then sobered when Zya appeared and snapped her fingers, making instruction sheets appear out of thin air. The tall brunette with long wavy hair held up her crochet hook and pointed at her yarn. The end started to wrap around her hook as she asked, "Are we ready to get started?"

Brinn nodded along with the rest of the group and found herself mesmerized by the woman's soothing voice. Zya was a new witch in town. Kind, mysterious, and very beautiful. No one really knew much about her other than she was from Salem and had moved to Keating Hollow for a fresh start. Brinn guessed most of the women who'd shown up for the class had done so more because they wanted to scope out Zya rather than learn a new stitch. But that would have to wait, because as Zya started explaining the multiple stitches they were going to learn, it was clear there wasn't going to be much time for gossip.

That would have to come later. Brinn quickly made a slipknot and got busy chaining her first row so that she could follow Zya's instructions.

CHAPTER 2

"*I*'ve got it," Austin said, pulling open the door to Witches in Stitches.

"Thank you, Austin." Caroline Carmichael gave him a grateful smile. "You're such a gentleman to walk me in. I promise I won't be too long."

He smiled down at his neighbor. "Take as long as you need. I'm not in any hurry." Austin had just taken his late grandmother's best friend out to lunch, and when she'd mentioned she needed some yarn for her latest project, he'd offered to stop so that she could check out the new store.

"You always were a sweet boy," Caroline said, hugging his arm.

"Don't go stroking my ego too much, Caroline. You don't want me to get a big head, do you?"

"If you do, you'll have to contend with my wooden spoon. You hear me?" she said, pointing a long, boney finger at him.

He just laughed. The wooden spoon threat was an old one. In all his years, she'd never made good on her promises.

"Caroline!" Ms. Betty called from across the room. "Looks

like you've found yourself a hottie. Bring that scrumptious piece of man-meat over here so we can ogle... I mean, say hello."

Austin shook his head as he followed his neighbor over to the gathering of women with their crochet hooks. Just as his gaze landed on Brinn, the gorgeous blonde let out a slight gasp and then glanced away, her cheeks bright pink.

"Ms. Betty, I think calling someone a piece of man-meat might be frowned upon these days," Wanda said, not unkindly.

"Right. I'm woke. I just forget myself sometimes." Ms. Betty stood and held her hand out to Austin. "Hello, there. Since I haven't seen you around these parts before, I assume you're new in town."

"Relatively new," Austin said, amused by the older woman. He'd heard of Ms. Betty. Caroline had described her as a colorful, fun-loving character, and despite her man-meat comment, Austin found her adorable. As he shook her hand, he added, "I'm Austin Steele. Caroline and my grandmother Peggy were best friends before she passed."

"Austin?" Ms. Betty yanked him to her and hugged him so tightly he let out an *oomph*. "I've heard so much about you. I'm so sorry for your loss. Peggy was a wonderful woman."

Austin gently pulled back and gave the woman a small smile. "Thank you. She is definitely missed."

Caroline put her arm through his and tugged him back away from Ms. Betty. "Well, ladies, it was nice to see you today. I better hurry and get my few things so I'm not keeping Austin here too long. He was kind enough to stop, and I don't want him to regret that decision."

"There's no chance of that," Austin said as he met Brinn's gaze.

"Oh... I see how it is," Ms. Betty whispered to Miss Maple.

The two women chatted quietly to each other while Austin tuned them out. Ms. Betty wasn't wrong. Her obvious assumption that he was interested in Brinn was exactly on target. She'd been his once, and he'd been stupid enough to let her go back then. If she'd just give him half a chance, he'd never make that mistake again. He nodded to her and asked, "Brinn, would you mind if I talked to you for a moment?"

Brinn cleared her throat. "I'm in the middle of a class, Austin," she said, holding up her crochet project. She was only a few rows deep, and whatever she was making really hadn't taken shape yet.

"I'll catch you up," Wanda said helpfully as she nudged Brinn in the side.

Brinn cast her an irritated glance before standing and making her way to Austin. She strode past him and right outside into the chilly January afternoon. Once Austin caught up to her, she put her hands on her hips and asked, "Did you know I was going to be here?"

Austin frowned as he shook his head. "How would I have known that?"

She let out an exaggerated huff. "I don't know. It's just that of all places to run into you again, I never thought it would be Witches in Stitches."

He let out a chuckle. "I have to agree with you there. This was an impromptu stop. Do you really think I'd stoop to stalking just to talk to you?"

Her cheeks flushed pink again, and she shook her head sheepishly. "No. I guess not." Then her expression turned calculating. "I'm pretty sure I made it clear we don't really have anything to say to one another. What do you want from me, Austin?"

"I…" Dammit. He knew what he wanted. But he couldn't

tell her that all he wanted was *her*. Not now. Not yet. There was too much history. Too much water under the bridge for them. He ran a hand through his hair and blew out a breath. "I want to apologize for the way I left five years ago."

Her features softened as if she hadn't been expecting his apology. "Okay. I appreciate that."

Austin could still hear the message she'd left on his voice mail when she'd found his note. The one that had just said, *I'm sorry*. He'd had his reasons, but he hadn't filled her in. He'd just packed his bags and left. How could he tell her that if he'd slowed down long enough to tell her his plans he'd have never left? And that would have destroyed him.

It hadn't been fair on his part, and he knew it wasn't fair to ask her forgiveness now, but he had no choice. He'd left his heart in Keating Hollow that day, and he'd never gotten it back.

"What I did—" Austin started.

Brinn quickly put up her hand, stopping him. "You don't need to do this, Austin. It's been a long time. Maybe we should just leave the past where it belongs."

His heart sank. This wasn't how he'd envisioned this conversation going. But really, he shouldn't be surprised. The last few times he'd tried to talk to her, she'd made it perfectly clear she wasn't interested in what he had to say. The fact that she was standing in front of him without stalking off was practically a miracle. "Can I at least take you out to lunch... as old friends?"

She gave him a sad smile. "We were never friends, Austin. We both know that."

"True." Their love affair had been intense from the start. "But it's been a number of years now. And since I'm back in Keating Hollow, it would be nice to not be enemies."

"We're not enemies," Brinn said softly. She reached out and

squeezed his hand, making him ache to pull her into his arms. But as soon as the thought flashed in his mind, she let go and added, "I just think we have too much history to pursue any sort of relationship outside of casual acquaintances. It's been really nice seeing you, Austin. But I should probably get back inside."

Austin watched her disappear back into the shop, feeling defeated. She'd made herself perfectly clear. He wasn't going to get into her good graces anytime soon, but at least they'd made progress and she hadn't stormed off again.

It was honestly more than he could've asked for, and he'd have to be satisfied with that for the time being.

Taking a deep breath, Austin followed her back into the shop to wait for Caroline. He walked toward the counter where Caroline was checking out, but he was hijacked by a small, older woman with bright red lipstick and a lowcut blouse.

"Hey there, handsome," she said, clutching his arm and batting her eyelashes at him.

While he hadn't placed her right away, her flirty tone triggered his memory. "What can I do for you, Ms. Betty?"

She took a moment to run her gaze over him as a sly smile claimed her lips. "Oh, honey, what couldn't you do for me?"

"Betty," Caroline warned from her spot near the register. "Behave yourself."

Ms. Betty laughed and then winked at Austin as she lowered her voice. "Caroline needs to lighten up. You give me a call when you're in the mood for some real fun, got it?"

Austin chuckled and shook his head at the outrageous woman. "How about you join us the next time I take Caroline to lunch?"

"Really?" she asked, her eyes sparking with delight. "That

would be lovely. I think I'll take you up on that. In the meantime, I hope I'll see you at the bachelorette auction this weekend. It's for a great cause."

Austin blinked at her. "Bachelorette auction?"

"Yes. You bid on one of our lovely bachelorettes, and when you win, you go on your date right after the event. The money is being used for Keating Hollow's new Artist in Residence program." She gave him a cheeky grin. "Brinn is going to be one of the bachelorettes."

"Brinn Taylor?" Had Austin heard the other woman correctly? Offering herself up for an auction seemed entirely out of character for Brinn. He glanced over at the couches and caught Brinn staring at him. She quickly turned her attention back to her project. Then he spotted Wanda Danvers grinning at him, and he knew that she must've put her cousin up to participating in the auction. And if the other women had gotten in on the conversation, Brinn would've said yes just because she didn't want to disappoint anyone.

"So you'll be there with a big load of cash?" Ms. Betty asked pointedly.

Would he? Austin was certain that Brinn didn't want him bidding on her. But he also knew her well and was just as certain that she wouldn't want to have to spend the day with a stranger. Still, he didn't want her thinking that he hadn't heard her or didn't respect her wishes to not see each other socially. Bidding on her wouldn't exactly be the gentlemanly thing to do.

"Austin?" Ms. Betty prompted. "There are, of course, other women who will be offering themselves up. Like me for example." She fluffed her white hair and twisted as if posing for the cameras.

He couldn't help it. Austin let out a bark of laughter and said, "With an invitation like that, how can I say no?"

"That's a good boy." She patted his chest and leaned in to give him a kiss on the cheek.

"Betty? Are you harassing my neighbor again?" Caroline said, coming to a stop beside them.

"Of course not." She pecked Caroline on the cheek as well and then waved her goodbyes as she hurried back over to the couches.

Caroline looked at him. "She didn't grope you or anything, did she?"

"Not this time," he said seriously and then smirked. "She did however invite me to bid on her at the bachelorette auction."

Caroline raised one eyebrow. "Are you going to?"

"I don't see why not." He winked at her. "It's for a good cause, and she seems like a good time."

"You're impossible. Both of you," she said, shaking her head. "Well, if you're going to bid, bid high. Otherwise we'll never hear the end of it. Bid high and often, okay?"

Austin patted his front pocket where he kept his wallet and nodded. "Got it."

"I bet you do," Caroline said as she walked out the door with Austin right behind her.

CHAPTER 3

"This was a bad idea," Brinn said as she stared out at the small gathering of mostly older men seated in front of the makeshift stage.

"Oh, come on. It's not that bad," Blake said as she applied her red lipstick.

"That's easy for you to say." Brinn glanced over at Cam Berry, one of the few guys under the age of sixty who was sitting in the back row, holding a sign with the number 28 on it. "You have the comfort of knowing someone you like is going to bid on you."

Blake's eyes twinkled. "It is nice of him, isn't it?"

"Nice?" Brinn guffawed. "That boy is half in love with you. I'm sure he's thrilled with the situation."

"No he isn't," she said, sounding thoroughly unconvincing. "We're just... good friends."

"If you say so," Brinn said and smoothed her red-velvet dress. The auction was being held in the event space at the Pelsh winery. All dates would be held directly afterward on the grounds. As usual, the Pelshes had gone all out. There was an enchanted carriage that would take guests out to the ice-skating rink, floating candles to light the room, and animated snowmen that were manning the magical chocolate bar.

The snowmen were pushing something called Holiday Cheer that was supposed to lift everyone's mood. Brinn wondered if she should've snagged one before the auction. Certainly she'd fetch a better price if she had an easy smile on her face. So far, she'd only managed a sad sort of grimace when she looked in the mirror.

"There you are!" Ms. Betty exclaimed as she made a beeline for Blake. "It's almost time, and you're up first."

"I'm ready." Blake stood back and opened her arms wide. "How do I look?"

Ms. Betty narrowed her eyes on the younger woman, taking in her long black skirt and black peasant blouse. "Like you're ready to lead a séance under the full moon. But there's no time to fix it now. Come on."

Brinn met Blake's gaze and they both chuckled. Blake looked incredible, though Brinn had to admit there was definitely a witchy vibe to her outfit. Especially since she'd paired the skirt with black lace-up boots. But so what? They were in Keating Hollow, a magical town. Everyone was a witch. Just not the kind who wore all black and looked like they worshipped at Elvira's alter. "Good luck," Brinn called after her.

"Apparently I'm going to need it," she said and hurried after Ms. Betty.

Brinn followed and watched from behind a privacy screen as Ms. Betty paraded Blake around the stage.

"Get your dolla, dolla bills out, boys, because they don't get better than this sweet peach," Ms. Betty said into a microphone.

Blake visibly cringed, and Brinn didn't blame her. Even though they'd signed up to sell their company for charity, there was no reason to make it weird. But it *was* Ms. Betty out there on the stage. What had Brinn expected?

"You're gonna need to get your Benjamins out," Ms. Betty called with a wide grin, "because we're starting the bidding at five dollars."

Blake leaned over and whispered something to Ms. Betty.

The older woman waved a flustered hand. "Oh, that was supposed to be Lincolns. Lincoln is on the five-dollar bill. But if you bid a Benjamin, I'm sure you won't be sorry."

Brinn snickered and then sobered when practically every man in the audience flashed his number.

"Oh, wow. Y'all are giving me life." Ms. Betty fanned herself and then started pointing randomly as the bids climbed quickly up to over a hundred dollars.

Blake's panicked expression made Brinn want to flee. The men from the retirement village were trying to spend their kids' inheritance just to spend the afternoon with Blake, who was more than three times their junior.

Brinn spotted Cam Berry in the audience. He was sitting next to his father Cameron, and the two had their heads bent together. After a moment, Cam stood up and waved a wad of bills. "Two hundred dollars!"

"Sold!" Blake said, pointing at him, her eyes wide with surprise even as a small relieved smile claimed her lips.

"But—" Ms. Betty started as the other men in the crowd let out frustrated groans.

"Well done, Cam!" Wanda called, cutting off whatever Betty was going to say as she strolled out onto the stage. "Now, who's the lucky lad out there that's going to win a date with me? I've got my golf cart washed and polished, and plenty of libations are chilling in the cooler."

The bidding war for Wanda was just as intense as the bidding on Blake. When the bidding came to a stop, Cameron finally stood and offered a bid twice as much as the highest offer.

Wanda beamed.

The crowd complained loudly about ringers in the auction and unfair bidding practices.

"Now, boys," Betty said sweetly. "There's nothing in the rules that says significant others can't bid however much they want to. If one of you have a higher offer, the bidding is still open."

No hands were raised.

"Are you sure? Wanda has quite a reputation. I'm sure she'll take you for the ride of your life."

Hoots and hollers filled the barn.

Wanda grabbed the mic and added, "On the golf cart, boys. Don't let Ms. Betty lead you into the gutter."

They all laughed, and when no one else made a final bid, Ms. Betty slapped a gavel on her podium, pointed at Cameron, and yelled, "Sold!"

Wanda grinned at her partner and strolled off the stage right into his arms.

Shaking her head at the ridiculousness of it all, Brinn chuckled to herself. But then Ms. Betty was calling her name, and all the amusement fled as nerves took over. She didn't have anyone in the audience waiting to overbid for her time. There was no telling who the winner would be. When the group at Witches in Stitches had talked her into this, she'd been imagining someone age appropriate. But when she looked out at the attendees, it was clear Ms. Betty had done the majority of her recruiting at the retirement village. If the winner was only twice her age, she'd be lucky.

"We have a special treat for you, boys," Ms. Betty said into her mic. "I'm sure you all know Brinn Taylor from Hollow Books. Not only is she a working woman, but she's also single. So there's no chance there's a ringer in the audience this time. Be ready to write a fat check, because this one is on the market!"

"Ms. Betty!" Brinn hissed. "I'm not a piece of meat."

Betty patted her arm and whispered back, "Relax, I'm just working the crowd. It gets the money flowing."

Relax? There was no chance of that.

Ms. Betty gave her a gentle nudge. "Go on. Walk around the stage. Show off a little bit."

Swallowing her irritation, Brinn walked stiffly around the stage, trying to force a smile. She'd get through this and then never participate again. What in the world had she been thinking?

"Who wants to start the bidding off?" Ms. Betty asked.

Only two numbers went up in the air, and Brinn's heart sank. Both Blake and Wanda had every man in the room bidding on them. But only two were interested in her? Good goddess, she couldn't even catch the interest of the retirement village men. That was it; she was destined to be alone forever.

"Fifty, seventy-five," Ms. Betty was calling to the crowd.

Brinn frowned and looked out into the audience again. More numbers were starting to creep into the air, and she let out a sigh of relief. It wasn't nearly as frenzied as the past two auctions, but plenty of men had started to participate. It just appeared they were being more strategic.

"One-twenty-five." Betty pointed at a man in the front row.

Brinn's gaze landed on him and then at the shadow of a

woman standing just behind him with her arms crossed and a scowl on her face. She was glaring at the man, but then she glanced up and met Brinn's stare. Her eyes widened in surprise for a moment before she shouted, "He's mine. You hear me? Stay away!"

Ghost.

The word ricocheted in her mind as her entire body went cold.

"Mine!" the ghost shouted again. A second later she disappeared into the ether.

CHAPTER 4

*A*ustin stood in the back of the barn, clutching the number he'd been handed when he walked inside. He wasn't exactly sure what had compelled him to attend the event. Sure, Ms. Betty had goaded him into it, but he also knew that the only woman he wanted to bid on absolutely did not want to be forced to spend the afternoon with him.

He'd planned to bid if there was anyone who wasn't getting the attention they deserved, but so far, that hadn't been an issue. And it certainly wasn't an issue for Brinn. Even though the bidding wasn't as frenzied as it had been in the beginning, it was steady and rising.

"One-twenty-five!"

Austin turned to see who was bidding over three figures, but froze when he saw Brinn's face. She'd gone completely white and looked as if she was ready to bolt right off the stage. Austin had no idea why Brinn had just gone into flight mode, but whatever it was, he couldn't just stand there and do nothing. Without a second thought, he raised his number. "Two hundred."

Brinn's head jerked up. It took her a moment to find him, but when her eyes landed on him, she let out a visible sigh of relief.

It was all the encouragement he needed. When the man in the front row bid again, Austin doubled it.

"Sold!" Ms. Betty called before the man could wave his number again, and Austin wondered if the older woman had also noticed Brinn's discomfort with the other man. "Aren't you the lucky one," Betty said as she winked at Brinn. "Keating Hollow's newest eligible bachelor just threw down some serious cash for an afternoon with you."

Brinn just gave her a weak smile and then turned her attention to the crowd, her gaze focusing on anything and everyone except Austin.

"Dammit," Austin muttered to himself. Brinn may have been happy he'd been there to save her in that moment, but she still clearly wasn't comfortable seeing him again. However, he wasn't going to let the opportunity go. This was his chance to truly apologize for the way he'd left town five years ago and give her the explanation she deserved.

After giving his donation for the auction, Austin waited in the back of the event hall for Brinn to appear. He watched as one by one, the participants were paired off and exited the barn until only the event organizers were left. Frowning, he walked over to where Ms. Betty was sitting behind a table and chattering about how much money they'd raised.

"Hello, Austin," she said, her eyes twinkling at him. "I bet you're excited about your date. You must be after plunking down that much cash."

He cleared his throat. "Yes, that's why I'm here. Have you seen Bri—"

"I'm here," Brinn said, seeming to appear out of nowhere.

Her lips were shiny with a fresh application of gloss, and her cheeks were flushed pink.

Was she blushing? He took a step toward her and her cheeks darkened. That was a definite yes. His lips split into a grin as he held his arm out to her. "You look lovely, Brinn."

His date averted her eyes and waved at Ms. Betty nervously. "See you at the next bitch and stitch session."

"Only if you're not monopolized by this gorgeous piece of man-meat," the older woman said with a wink.

Brinn groaned, making Austin chuckle.

"It was nice to see you again, Ms. Betty," he said, giving her a cheeky grin.

"You, too!" She fluffed her hair and wiggled her fingers at him. "Don't be a stranger now, you hear? There's happy hour at the pool over at the retirement village every Thursday at five. I'd love it if you were my guest."

"Will this never end?" Brinn muttered under her breath.

Austin chuckled. "January might be a little cool for hanging out at the pool. Ask me again when the weather warms up."

"It's heated!" she called after them.

Austin just waved as he led Brinn away from the feisty woman.

Brinn looked up at him. "You know that just encourages her, right?"

"Sure, but she's fun," he said lightheartedly. "So who's to say I won't join her for happy hour one day?"

"You just wait until you're trapped in the pool by Ms. Betty and her friends. Saggy bikinis and all. Then we'll see how much fun you're having."

The visual was more than Austin had bargained for, but still, he laughed at the idea of him in the pool with the retirees. "Perhaps I'll have to rethink her invitation."

Brinn shook her head. "Good luck with that. I'm sure she'll remind you of it every chance she gets."

"Probably." Austin had no doubt that was true. But Ms. Betty didn't scare him. He knew a little flattery would get him out of pretty much anything. He glanced around at the almost empty venue and then nodded toward the door. "Are you ready?"

"For what?" she asked, staring up at him with wide eyes.

"Our date?" He raised one eyebrow. "You weren't planning on ditching me, were you?"

Brinn straightened her shoulders and looked him right in the eye. "No, I think that's your MO, not mine."

Ouch. He'd walked right into that one. Austin cleared his throat. "Right. Then how about we take a walk around the property?"

"Sure." She swept past him, her long blond hair swinging down her back.

Austin followed her out the door and smiled to himself as she slipped a black knit cap with cat ears over her head. It was the one he'd given to her six years ago for Christmas. He knew it probably meant nothing, but he couldn't help hoping she thought of him every time she wore it. Before he could stop himself, he said, "Nice hat."

She let out an irritated huff. "Don't read anything into it. I just like the cat ears."

"I know." It was the reason he'd purchased it for her. Brinn was a huge cat lover. She was the type of girl who wore *Cat Mom* T-shirts and was a sucker for every stray cat in the neighborhood. He wouldn't be surprised to find she'd adopted a couple more since he'd left town. "How's Buffy?"

"Buffy's perfect, thank you," she said, turning to smile at

him. "She's probably lounging in a patch of sun on my bed as we speak."

"Or ripping up your pillow," he teased.

"No, she's past that stage. But I wouldn't put it past Xander. He's a real terror when he's been cooped up too long. And since it's been cold, I haven't let him out for the past few days."

"Xander?" he asked. "When did he adopt you?"

"The same day Willow came into my life."

He let out a bark of laughter. "Do you have an Angel and Cordelia, too?"

"No. Besides, my next cat will be named Spike." Brinn had gone through a phase where she'd consumed every vampire novel and television show she could find. The camp of *Buffy the Vampire Slayer* had charmed her, and it hadn't taken long before she'd talked Austin into binging the entire series with her.

"Of course he will," Austin said. Spike had always been Brinn's favorite vampire.

Brinn paused near a row of wine grapes and looked up at him. "And how's Oz? Did he come with you to Keating Hollow?"

Austin nodded. "He's here, and I'm sure he'd love to see you."

Her smile faded as she glanced down at her feet. "I'm not sure that's a good idea."

"Brinn…" He couldn't help the small sigh that escaped his lips.

"What?" she asked him, her eyes narrowed. "Am I supposed to feel guilty because I don't want to see your dog? Because after you left, I not only grieved for our relationship, but also because you never even let me say goodbye to him? The Lhasa puppy that I helped you pick out, train, and love on for two years?"

"I—" Austin started, but she put her hand up, stopping him.

"Did it ever occur to you that maybe it's just too hard for me to see him when I know you're just going to take him away again? That it's really freakin' hard to stand here and talk to you like you didn't rip my heart out when you just walked out of my life without so much as an explanation? Like I meant so little to you that all I deserved was a stupid note? No phone call. No goodbyes. No anything. Just a broken heart and shattered dreams. But please, take me to your house so I can love all over Oz while you pretend that none of it ever happened!"

Austin took a deep breath, knowing he deserved every word of her tirade. "I owe you an apology and—"

"You're damned right you do, not that it's going to do any good. You can't change the past." She crossed her arms over her chest and glared at him.

"And..." Austin stressed, "I'd like to at least explain my actions." He grabbed her right hand and held it in both of his. "Would you do me the small favor of at least listening? When I've gotten everything out, I'll go and let you out of this date."

Brinn stared down at their joined hands and then squeezed her eyes shut. "I waited a long time for an explanation, but now that you're offering, I'm not sure I want to hear it."

Dammit. Where did Austin go from here? He didn't want to offer excuses. Instead, he wanted to make it clear that she hadn't done anything wrong. His decision to leave had been a difficult choice, but one he'd made so that he wouldn't destroy them both. Glancing around, he spotted a wooden bench tucked among the vines.

Gently, he tugged her toward the bench and asked, "Can we

sit for a minute?" Without answering, she sat, staring out at the vineyard. Austin joined her and said in a quiet voice, "I'm sorry I hurt you."

A tiny flinch registered on Brinn's face before she schooled herself, still refusing to look at him. He didn't blame her. If she'd left him the way he'd left her, he likely wouldn't have forgiven her either.

"There was stuff going on with my dad that I never told you about," he said, not quite sure where to start.

Her gaze flicked to his as her brows pinched together. "What do you mean?"

This was the moment of truth where he laid it all on the line and hoped she understood not only why he'd left, but also why he'd never told her the details. He swallowed the resentment in his throat and decided to start at the beginning. "You know my dad was a business consultant, right?"

"Sure. Something to do with helping startups find angel investors, right?"

"Yes. He also helped with structuring startups, but that was his main job. He worked for shares in the private companies, hoping that they'd go public so he could cash in."

Brinn nodded. "It must've paid off at least some of the time. It looked like he did pretty well for himself."

"Yeah." There was bitterness in Austin's tone and a familiar uneasiness in his gut that always materialized when he talked about his father. "He got lucky a few times, and he cashed in."

"There's nothing wrong with that, is there?" she asked, sounding confused.

"No. Not on the surface there isn't." Austin felt a muscle tick as his jaw tightened. "But after his net worth went up, he changed. You must've wondered why I introduced you to my grandmother but never my father."

Brinn's eyes flashed with something he couldn't quite read. Anger? Annoyance? Frustration? But the emotion disappeared just as fast as it had materialized. "I just figured he was busy."

Her tone was nonchalant, but Austin saw through it. The emotion in her eyes had been pain. He'd hurt her by not introducing her to his dad. Still, he stood by his decisions. Nothing good would have come from introducing them. "He was, but there was another reason why I didn't want him to know you."

"Why?" This time there was no mistaking the anger in her fiery eyes. "Was I not good enough for him? Would he have been mad that his golden boy was interested in a townie?"

"Brinn," Austin said, taking her hand in both of his again. "No. None of your assumptions are accurate, though I can see why you might think that. I didn't introduce you to him because I was trying to protect you. I never told you this, but my father turned into a drunk. The mean kind who would do just about anything to get his way. He did it with his clients, his girlfriend, and me. The only person he wasn't able to push around was my grandmother. She never stood for it, and for some reason, he respected her for it. The rest of us? We didn't stand a chance. I didn't want you in his crosshairs."

Brinn frowned. "So what are you saying? That he'd have used me to get to you?"

"Yes."

"To do what?"

"Join his company. He wanted me to be his partner, to clean up the messes he created after he emptied his liquor cabinet."

"But you were a musician," she said. "Not a suit. Even if he did need someone to take over for him when he was... um, incapacitated, you didn't know anything about angel investing. What exactly did he want you to do?"

"Whatever he told me to do, I guess. He thought music was a dead-end career," Austin said with a shrug. "At least that was his line after he started drinking every day. When I was younger he was supportive. On his worst days, he'd insist that if I was determined to keep on trying to make a go of it with my guitar that I'd end up on a street corner, begging for food money."

Brinn snorted. "I guess you showed him since you now own the most successful recording studio in LA."

Austin had grown up playing multiple musical instruments and had long dreamed of playing in a band. But as he got older, his interests had shifted to music producing. When he'd left Keating Hollow for LA, he'd done so with his grandmother's blessing. And with her help, he'd eventually opened his own recording studio. He'd had early success producing a friend's debut album, and things had snowballed from there. "Things did manage to work out for me, but before I left Keating Hollow, he tried everything he could think of to strong-arm me into his business."

"Like what?" she asked, her eyes narrowing again. He knew that look. She always wore that fierce expression when she was ready to defend someone. His heart beat a little faster at the thought of her caring enough to get riled up on his behalf.

"He tried to sabotage my internship," Austin said. The summer before he'd left town for good, he'd had a four-week internship at a studio in New York. "He also managed to get my credit card cut off while I was there, hoping I'd ask him for help. When I contacted my grandmother, he called, accusing me of using her. It was a lot of garbage like that."

"So you left because of your dad?" she asked.

"Yes." Austin let out a relieved breath. "That's exactly it. I needed to get away from him. It was never because I wanted to leave you."

Brinn pressed her lips into a thin line as she pulled her hand out of his and shifted to put more space between them. "Fine. But I always knew you were going to end up in LA or New York or somewhere other than Keating Hollow. What I don't understand is why you didn't just tell me." She swallowed hard. "Or ask me to go with you."

He could have talked to her. Probably should have, and the knowledge weighed heavily on his heart. But he'd had his reasons. "He made other threats... ones that involved you."

Brinn blinked. "What?"

Austin leaned back against the bench and closed his eyes. "One night when he was drunk off his ass, he made vague references about making it harder for your grandmother here. He threatened to evict your grandma from her café space." His father owned the building her grandmother had rented, and there was no question he'd have found a way evict her if he really wanted to. "I wasn't sure if he'd go through with it or if he even remembered the threat, but he's been known to be ruthless in some of his business dealings before, so I couldn't say it was just idle talk. At the time, I believed he might've followed through with his threats."

"He wanted to mess with my gran's café?" Brinn stood and started to pace in front of him. "Seriously? All because he couldn't handle that you didn't want to work with him?"

"Yes. He needed someone who would cover for him before his business contacts all turned on him. I couldn't do that if I was starting a music career."

She stopped pacing and stared at him. "I still don't know why you just didn't tell me."

"Because it was during that conversation that I made up my

mind about moving, and since I knew you never wanted to leave Keating Hollow... I just packed that night. The next morning as I walked out the door, I told him we'd broken up and that I was leaving for good. It was the best way to take his focus off you and your grandmother."

"So you decided on your own what was best for me?" She shook her head. "Don't you think my grandma and I deserved to know that your dad was threatening our livelihood?"

Austin stood and placed both hands on her shoulders, holding her gaze. "Brinn, I was a young man, desperate to break away from my father. I had no idea if his talk was just drunken threats or if he really meant it, but at that point, his addiction was escalating, and I didn't want either of you caught in his manipulation and lies. I thought I was being noble and protecting you. I knew if I broke ties with you that he'd leave you alone. It wasn't about you; it was about controlling me. When he realized we were no longer together and I was already gone, using you as leverage was no longer advantageous to him. I probably handled it all wrong, but I did love you."

Brinn stared up at him, her eyes shining with unshed tears. "Your father is an ass. But that was no excuse for the way you left or the silence that followed."

He nodded. "You're right. I didn't call because I knew if I did, I'd never have been able to stay away." His hands tightened on her arms, and he couldn't stop himself from pulling her closer to him. When her breath caught, all rational thought fled his mind, and he bent his head, brushing his lips over hers for the first time in over five years.

CHAPTER 5

*B*rinn's arms wrapped around Austin and she melted into him. The kiss threw her back in time, and for the moment, she forgot all the hurt and anguish she'd suffered the past five years as she longed for this man she'd loved with all her heart.

Austin's warmth enveloped her, and she opened for him, welcoming his kiss and the hint of coffee on his tongue. Everything inside her just felt *right*. All the chaos of the world had stopped, and she was exactly where she was supposed to be... in the arms of the man she'd never stopped loving.

"Brinn," he murmured as he pulled back just a touch.

Her eyelids fluttered open and she stared into his whiskey-colored eyes.

"Damn, I've missed you."

His words shocked her into action, and she quickly took a step back, putting distance between them. When he tried to move forward, she put her hand up, stopping him. "No, Austin. We can't do this."

He raised both eyebrows in question. "Why? Are you seeing someone?"

If only, she thought. That would certainly make this easier. But Brinn wasn't going to lie. That wasn't in her nature. "No, I'm not. I just... We can't act like nothing happened. Falling back into your arms just because you explained why you left isn't smart."

Austin lifted his hand and tucked a lock of her long blond hair behind her ear. "Maybe it isn't smart, but it feels right, doesn't it?"

Yes. "No." Brinn shook her head. "We can't just pick up where we left off, Austin. It doesn't work like that."

He shoved his hands into his pockets and stared at the ground for a moment. When he looked up, he nodded. "Okay. I hear you."

Disappointment flooded through Brinn, and she forced back a scowl. She hated that he had that effect on her after all the time that had passed. Why hadn't she ever moved on from this man? She stepped out onto the path and paused as she looked back at him. "Can we try to be friends?"

"I'd like that," he said and moved to stand next to her. "We don't have to finish this date if you don't want to. I only bid because you seemed uncomfortable with the man bidding on you."

The vision of the female ghost flashed in her mind, and she grimaced at the memory. It had been a long time since she'd seen a ghost, and the experience wasn't welcome. Especially not in Keating Hollow, the town that had always been her sanctuary.

Austin's expression turned fierce as he asked, "Did that man do something to you?"

"What? No." She shook her head. "It wasn't anything like that."

He blew out a long breath. "Good. That's good." Then he frowned. "Want to tell me what was going on there? Or was it just the entire auction experience you regretted?"

She let out a huff of laughter. "You could say that. Once I was onstage, all I wanted to do was exit stage left immediately. I think it's safe to say that a bachelorette style auction is not for me, even if it is for a good cause." Brinn gave him a halfhearted smile and added, "Thank you for saving me from an awkward date with a man more than twice my age and his dead wife."

"You're welcome—wait, dead wife?"

Brinn started to walk as she nodded. "The ghost of his wife was standing behind him, and she wasn't happy he was bidding on me for a date."

Austin kept pace with her as they moved down the path that led them toward another field of vines. "You actually saw her ghost? Here in Keating Hollow?"

"Yes," Brinn said with a sigh.

"Has this happened before?"

"Nope. Never. Only when I leave Keating Hollow." It was why Brinn never wanted live anywhere other than her home town. Brinn had grown up in Keating Hollow, and it wasn't until she'd left for college that she realized she was a medium. She'd spent all four years plagued by ghosts who wanted to tell her their stories. They'd exhausted her. And in a few cases, terrified her. She'd come home right after graduation, and her peaceful life had returned, cementing the fact that she had no desire to ever live anywhere else.

Since her father had died when Brinn was young and her mother had skipped town when Brinn was eighteen, Brinn had moved in with her paternal grandmother after she'd returned from college and helped out at her café until her grandmother's death. It had been rough losing her. And since she'd inherited her grandmother's house, Brinn was constantly surrounded by her memory. Her grandmother had been her favorite person in the world. Her only person, really, besides Wanda. And she missed her terribly.

"That's disconcerting," Austin said, referring to the sudden appearance of a ghost. "Maybe it's just because the Pelsh winery is out in the country," he speculated.

"Maybe. I hope so." Brinn's palms turned clammy as her anxiety spiked.

Austin closed his hand around hers and squeezed gently.

Brinn appreciated his silent support and that he didn't offer any empty words of reassurance. He'd somehow always known exactly what she needed. Tears burned the backs of her eyes, but she turned her head and blinked them back. The last thing she was going to do was cry in front of him today. She pulled her hand from his, needing a little bit of space, but then turned abruptly and stared him in the eye as she asked, "How long are you going to be here in Keating Hollow?"

He seemed taken aback by her outburst as he just stared at her, looking stunned for a moment. But then a small smile claimed his lips as he asked, "How long do you want me to stay?"

"Seriously?" Brinn's irritation flared to life, and with a shake of her head, she muttered, "Never mind." Then she stalked off in the direction of the parking lot and called over her shoulder, "The date's over."

"Brinn!"

She didn't look back as she held her hand up, indicating their conversation and the fake date was officially over. Because Brinn was not going to stand there and let the man who broke her heart flirt with her as if nothing had ever happened. Not today. Not ever. And especially not since he didn't live in Keating Hollow. Because even though he'd been in town for a few months, she knew he'd eventually return to LA and leave just like everyone else in her life. She should've been used to it, but that pain never fully went away, and she wasn't eager to experience it again.

"GOOD MORNING, BRINN," Yvette called from behind the coffee bar at Hollow Books.

Brinn waved at her as she tucked her belongings under the counter at the register. Without saying a word, she made her way to the storage room and was grateful to find over a dozen boxes of books that needed to be unloaded, scanned, and shelved. After getting almost no sleep the night before, she wasn't in the mood to deal with customers, no matter how pleasant or friendly they usually were.

With a box knife in hand, she went to work opening up the latest shipment.

Ten minutes later, Yvette, her boss and the store owner, appeared in the doorway. She was holding a cup of coffee and a paper plate with two pieces of pumpkin bread. "I brought you breakfast."

Brinn eyed the pumpkin bread then met Yvette's concerned gaze. "Thanks."

Yvette placed the coffee and plate on the small table near the door. "Want to talk about it?"

No. Not at all. But when she went to shake her head, she nodded instead and sat down on the concrete floor next to one of the open boxes. "Dammit. Why did he have to come back here?"

Yvette took a seat in a plastic chair and said, "I assume you mean Austin."

Brinn waved an impatient hand. "Who else?"

The dark-haired beauty let out a chuckle. "It looks to me like there's a second chance romance blooming."

"No. No way. Never going to happen," Brinn insisted as she glared at her boss.

Yvette shrugged one shoulder. "If you say so, but most people don't protest that much unless they're trying to convince themselves."

Groaning, Brinn pressed a hand to her eyes. "Why are you torturing me?"

"For entertainment. When you spend most of your days with a ten-month-old and a petulant toddler, adult interaction is priceless."

Brinn peeked out from behind her hand. "Is Skye still having trouble adjusting?"

"A little bit. She loves her little brother, but she's so used to being the center of attention that there's a little competition there. Her favorite thing to do when I'm feeding Toby is to scream at the top of her lungs and run around throwing her Elmo at the wall. The poor thing. It's a miracle he hasn't lost a limb yet."

"I'm sure she'll grow out of it," Brinn said, giving her a sympathetic smile. "Sibling rivalry is completely normal."

She sighed. "I know. It's just so hard to see our sweet girl acting out like that. We have made a point of making sure she gets one-on-one time with both of us each night. It's just a lot, you know?"

Brinn nodded, though she didn't really know. She didn't

have kids, nor did she have any siblings. But Keating Hollow was experiencing a sort of baby boom, especially with the Townsend sisters, so she'd heard enough to be familiar with the growing pains. "How's Toby?"

Yvette's eyes sparkled as she gave Brinn a soft smile. "He's lovely. Such a sweet child. I don't know how we got so lucky, but we adore him."

A pang of longing hit Brinn, surprising her. She'd never really thought much about having children. It was always one of those "someday" type of things. But sitting there with Yvette, seeing how content and settled she was with Jacob and her growing family, it made her long for something more than the life she was living. "That's really wonderful, Yvette. You need to bring him by sometime soon so I can kiss those sweet cheeks of his."

"I will," she promised and then stood with her hands on her hips. "Enough about me. Tell me about your auction date with Austin. How did it go?"

Brinn pulled a pile of books out of the box in front of her and said, "It went... okay, I guess. He apologized for the way things went down when he left five years ago and did some explaining."

"And...?" she asked, an expectant look on her face.

"And what?" Brinn stared up at her.

"Well, did his explanation change anything? Will you see him again? Did you get some closure? Give me *something*," she teased.

Brinn sighed and leaned back against the wall. "No, it didn't really change anything, but at least I know what happened and why. Closure?" She laughed. "I doubt we'll ever have closure. And will I see him again? I guess. As long as he's in Keating Hollow, it's inevitable, right?"

Yvette's shoulders slumped in disappointment. "He could have at least asked you out again. On a real date, not a charity auction one."

Shaking her head, Brinn said, "That wouldn't have gone over well. Not with the way we ended things."

"Oh." Yvette gave her a sympathetic smile. "I guess things are still a little raw. Well," she added with a wave of her hand. "You never know what the future will bring. Right?"

"Right," Brinn agreed and hated that a small bubble of hope blossomed in her chest. No matter how much she wanted to deny it, she really did want to see Austin again. She wanted him to ask her to dinner. But what would she do when he left again? The bubble of hope popped, leaving her feeling empty and frustrated. "I should get to work on these books. They aren't going to stock themselves."

Yvette nodded. "It's time to flip the open sign anyway. Let me know if you want a break from stocking. We can switch jobs for a while."

"I'm sure I'll be fine," Brinn said. "But thanks."

Yvette waved as she disappeared from the stockroom, leaving Brinn alone with the books and her thoughts. She squeezed her eyes shut and shook her head, trying to get Austin out of her mind.

The gesture was useless, though. Because for the next hour, all she did was wonder what she would have said if Austin had asked her to leave town with him. She wanted to believe she'd have said yes, but deep down she knew she wouldn't have. Her life at college had been full of ghosts following her around, trying to talk to her. Some were benign and just happy to chat, while others insisted on her sending messages to their loved ones. And the worst ones were the spirits who'd died a violent death and were either out of their minds or desperate to get

44

revenge on their killers. For a young woman who was already dealing with the trauma of her mother walking out on her, it had been far more than she could handle. Dealing with ghosts again was something she just didn't know if she could face. Leaving Keating Hollow wasn't an option, not even for Austin Steele.

Once Brinn was done scanning all the books, she loaded a cart, pushed it out into the store, and rounded the corner into one of the aisles. Just as she paused near the paranormal mystery section, movement caught her eye. She glanced up just in time to see her grandmother smiling at her. Her breath got caught in her throat, and tears stung her eyes. The woman who'd passed away four years ago waved and then vanished into thin air.

CHAPTER 6

*A*ustin sat at his grandmother's desk, staring down at her trust. He'd read it no less than a dozen times, but still read it again, trying to find some answers. It didn't make sense. His grandmother had left his father a small sum of money, left her house to Austin, and the rest of her assets were split between him and Gideon Alexander.

He read the name again. *Gideon Alexander*. The man was a former movie producer, turned artist. He was the son of Throm Alexander, a cutthroat power-player in the movie industry. Austin had no earthly idea why his grandmother would leave any part of her estate to a stranger, much less such a large portion of it.

As far as he could tell, they hadn't known each other. There wasn't any evidence of communication between the two. His number wasn't in her phone or the phonebook she'd still kept. There weren't any cards or letters or correspondence.

Austin knew Gideon had left his career in Hollywood and now owned an art gallery in town and was engaged to the writer Miranda Moon. He'd also been out of town on vacation for the past few weeks, so Austin hadn't had the opportunity to talk to him. He grabbed the phone and dialed the gallery.

A woman answered and said, "Enchanted K Gallery, how can I help you today?"

"Hello. Is Gideon Alexander in?" Austin asked.

"Not at the moment. Can I take a message?"

Austin bit back a curse. "That's all right. Can you tell me when he might be in again?"

"After lunch today," she offered.

"Perfect. I'll just stop by later. Thank you for your time." Austin put the phone down and sat back in the chair. It was the moment of truth. He was finally going to find out why his grandmother left money to someone she apparently didn't even know.

As he was filing the paperwork back into the desk, the phone rang. It was the house phone. No one from his life in LA would call him on that phone. If it was his studio manager or one of his friends, they'd call him on his cell phone.

Whoever it was, the call was likely about settling the trust. The estate attorney was anxious to send a notice to Gideon, but Austin had asked her to wait. He just felt the need to talk to the man first and make sure this wasn't some sort of elder scam. Had Gideon befriended his grandmother and convinced her to change her will? It was possible, though even Austin found that hard to believe. Everything he'd heard about Gideon Alexander had implied that the man wasn't hurting for money.

On the fourth ring, Austin grabbed the phone. "Hello?"

"Austin! I'm glad I caught you," his father said, his voice booming over the phone.

Austin's grip tightened on the receiver. "Dad, what can I do for you?"

Laughter filtered over the line. "What can you do for me? Is that anyway to greet your father, whom you haven't talked to in over a month?"

"Sorry, Dad. I've been a little busy dealing with Grandma's estate."

"Well, that's what I'm calling about. I'm about a week away from finishing up my current project, and when I'm done, I'm heading to Keating Hollow to help you deal with my mother's things. Won't that be great? I haven't seen you in ages."

Austin sat there, stunned. His grandmother had passed over two months ago, and in all that time, his father hadn't mentioned anything about coming back to Keating Hollow. Austin had been grateful. Now he was going to have to figure out how to coexist with the man for who knew how long.

"Austin? Did you hear me? Get the guestroom ready. I'll be there in eight days."

"Yeah. I heard you," Austin said and cleared his throat when he had trouble forcing the words out. "But you don't need to do that. I've got it covered. Really."

"Oh, come on now," he said. "I can't just leave it all on your shoulders. Besides, I'm sure you can use help closing out the estate."

"I—"

"The other line is ringing. Sorry, Son. I've got to go. See you next week."

The line went dead, and Austin threw it back down on the receiver, his frustration making him stand and pace the room. He hadn't spent any significant time with his father since the day he'd left Keating Hollow five years ago. It'd taken over two years before they'd even spoken. And that was only because his father had tracked him down in LA to make amends. In those two years, he'd lost his business and eventually found AA.

Austin had accepted his father's apologies and appreciated the gesture, but he hadn't forgiven him. There were some things that one just couldn't come back from with an apology.

"Dammit," he muttered and then stopped in his tracks when he spotted movement across the room. The hair stood up on his arms, and suddenly he had the feeling that he wasn't alone. "Hello?"

Cool air materialized, wafting over him and ruffling a piece of paper lying on the desk.

"Grandma?" he whispered, certain that if anyone was visiting from the other side, it was her.

The room was still.

"If you're here, give me another sign," he tried.

The clock ticked loudly in the otherwise silent room. Austin waited for a few minutes, then blew out a breath and ran a hand through his hair before stalking out of the office, feeling strangely like he'd lost his grandmother all over again.

AUSTIN WALKED along the cobblestone sidewalk down Main Street, his head down, ignoring the magical window displays that made Keating Hollow so special. Since the beginning of January, the bookstore had rotating quotes materializing on the glass, and the café had an animated snow scene that changed with the time of day. Most days he'd take the time to marvel at the creativity, but that afternoon, he was single-minded.

He had to get the trust settled before his dad showed up, or else he knew there'd be trouble. There was no doubt his father would get in the middle of it and make Austin's life hell in the process.

The paintings in the windows of the Enchanted K Gallery were bright, colorful depictions of Keating Hollow and full of whimsy. They were just the type of paintings his grandmother would've loved. Austin took a moment to look them over. There was one of Main Street, highlighting the Keating Hollow Inn. He imagined it would appeal to a tourist visiting the magical town. The other one was a landscape of the river and off in the distance were two golf carts that appeared to be racing, each of them full of women holding cocktail glasses and laughing with their hair flying in the wind. Austin chuckled. He'd heard of the epic golf cart races that Brinn's cousin Wanda often participated in. This was a painting for the locals.

The door opened and a couple walked out clutching a framed print. The woman was chattering about the exact place she was going to hang her newest piece of art. Her partner just nodded and grabbed her hand as they strolled down the street toward Incantation Café. It was late January, the coldest time of the year, and still the tourists flocked to Keating Hollow. It was just that inviting. In fact, even though Brinn had said she knew Austin would always leave one day, *he* hadn't always known that. He'd intended the town to be his home base. But then his father had made that impossible, and he'd had to get out.

Now that his father had moved, maybe that wasn't so impossible anymore. Maybe once he settled his grandmother's estate, he'd be able to decide if he wanted to make a life change.

Austin walked into the gallery. The pieces inside were just as vibrant as the ones in the window, and he was instantly impressed.

"Good afternoon," the man behind the counter said. "Gorgeous day out there, isn't it?"

Austin nodded. Despite the chilly temperature, the sun was shining and there was a whisper of new life in the air. It made it seem as if spring wasn't that far off. "It really is." He walked over to the counter. "You're Gideon Alexander, right?"

The man smiled at him. "In the flesh. What can I do for you?"

"You're a hard man to track down."

Gideon eyed him with curiosity. "Not usually. But tell me, Mr.—"

"Steele. But call me Austin," Austin said.

"Okay. Well then, Austin, why were you trying to track me down?"

Austin glanced around the gallery and then back at Gideon. "Did you happen to know Peggy Steele?"

Gideon's brows pinched together as he appeared to try to process Austin's question. Then his expression cleared. "Sure, I knew her. In fact, I painted that piece for her." He nodded to one of his whimsical paintings that hung behind him on the wall.

Austin recognized the scene instantly. It was the mountain view from his grandmother's kitchen window. He was touched, but then his feelings morphed to one of suspicion. "Did she commission that?"

"No. Not officially. But she did mention she'd love a painting of her mountain one day. I was intending to surprise her with it, but then she passed on. I'm really sorry for your loss." Gideon turned, pulled the painting off the wall, and handed it to Austin. "I'd like for you to have it. It wouldn't be right to sell it to someone else."

Austin tried to hand it back. "Oh, no. I couldn't. That's too much."

"It's not. I painted it for her," Gideon said, refusing to take it back. "Please. I'd really like you to have it."

Why? Who was this man to his grandmother? Austin just nodded and placed the painting against the counter. "Can I ask you something else?"

"Of course."

"How well did you know my grandmother?" Austin tried to keep his tone curious, and hoped the other man didn't pick up on his suspicion.

"Not well to be honest. I only met her a few times when she and her neighbor Caroline came in. I remembered her because she was so enamored with my new series. I was really sorry to hear of her passing. She was… vibrant."

"She was," Austin agreed, not sure what to make of the other man's answer. He'd learned that although Gideon hadn't been in Keating Hollow for long, he'd already earned the respect of the other residents.

Gideon studied Austin for a few moments as if trying to figure him out. Then he asked, "Why?"

"Why what?" Austin asked.

"Why did you want to know if I knew Peggy?"

Right. He hadn't wanted to tell the other man about his grandmother's will just yet, but not only did he have a moral obligation, he also needed to get it done before his father blew into town. He cleared his throat. Austin met the other man's gaze, watching carefully for any reaction. "As it turns out, I'm the executor of my grandmother's estate, and I'm here to inform you that she left you a sizable inheritance."

Gideon blinked, and then he frowned. "I'm sorry, what?"

Austin pulled an envelope out of his pocket and handed it to the other man. "The details are in here."

"I don't understand," Gideon said as his fingers tightened around the envelope.

There was no mistaking Gideon's confusion. The man hadn't been expecting Austin's news. That was obvious. Austin gave him a wry smile. "That makes two of us."

CHAPTER 7

$\mathcal{A}$ustin left The Enchanted K Gallery more perplexed than when he'd arrived. Gideon seemed like an upstanding man who was as caught off guard by the inheritance as Austin had been. He desperately wished there was some way to communicate with his grandmother.

You could ask Brinn. As soon as the thought formed in his head, Austin dismissed it. Austin knew better than anyone that Brinn never wanted to see or talk to another ghost. Not even Peggy Steele. She'd told him all about how her college years had been plagued with ghosts demanding her help. It had been completely overwhelming and sometimes downright traumatic. When a spirit demanded that Brinn needed to find her killer, that was just more than anyone should have to handle.

No, he would not ask Brinn. He'd just have to keep digging through his grandmother's paperwork to find out why she'd left a bunch of her money to a man she barely knew.

Before he even knew where he was heading, Austin found himself standing in front of Hollow Books. Words written in golden script scrolled across the glass of one of the windows. The other one featured a Miranda Moon novel that was open with wolves materializing from the pages and running off into the woods.

"It's really cute, right?" a woman asked from behind him.

Austin turned to find a pretty brunette dressed in a long black skirt and a purple corset. Her long, curly hair that was a little wild and her multiple silver rings and bracelets completed her mysterious, witchy look. Austin smiled warmly at her. "It's definitely eye-catching."

"Mary Pelsh helped me with it. She's a genius air witch. I'm constantly amazed at what she can do."

"You're Miranda Moon, right?" Austin asked.

"Sure am. How'd you know?"

"I saw your picture on the back of your book jacket," he said.

She grinned and held her hand out. "Does that mean you picked up my latest release? Yvette was kind enough to feature it for me."

"Not yet, but I'll be sure to grab one." Austin shook her hand. "Austin Steele. Nice to meet you."

"You, too. And thanks. I appreciate the support. Are you a new resident or just visiting Keating Hollow?"

He shrugged. "I'm not really sure yet."

She chuckled. "I've been there before. Though it didn't take much to convince me to move here. It's a special place."

"There's no doubt about that," Austin agreed.

She eyed him for a moment. "You're a lifer. You might not know it yet, but I can tell. By this time next year, you'll have made the move permanent." She patted his arm. "Trust me on this one."

Austin raised both eyebrows. "How can you be so sure?"

"I just know things." She winked and pulled the door open. "Are you headed in?"

He nodded, knowing that Brinn was inside. She was like a magnet. Walking away before he spoke to her wasn't an option. He backed up a step and gestured for Miranda to go in first.

She nodded her thanks and swept into the bookstore, her arms open in a grand gesture. "The bestselling resident author has arrived," she announced with a laugh.

Brinn's eyes glittered with amusement as she grinned at the author. "Hey, Miranda. We weren't expecting you today."

"I came to sign some books." She waved at Austin. "Look who I found milling around outside."

Brinn's gaze landed on him, and her smile faded. "Austin. Hello."

"Hello," he said, ignoring the disappointment gnawing at his gut. What he wouldn't give to see her eyes light up when he walked into a room.

"Uh... what are you... I mean, can I help you find anything?"

Austin gave her a hopeful smile, determined to break through her defenses. "Thanks," he said, walking toward her. "But I've already found what I'm looking for."

Her cheeks flushed pink.

His smile widened.

"Oh, wow," Miranda said, fanning herself. "Did the temperature shoot up in here, or is it just me?"

Brinn turned her attention to the author. "Miranda, your books are stocked on that front table over there."

Miranda laughed. "That's a very polite way of telling me to mind my own business. Don't worry, I got the message. Can I give a word of advice?"

"You're going to anyway, aren't you?" Brinn asked.

Miranda just smiled and then glanced at Austin. "This one likes you. That's obvious. Make sure you get dinner out of him before you let him down."

"Let me down?" he echoed in mock annoyance. "Whose side are you on, Miranda?"

"Brinn's. Always." She wiggled her fingers at them and then crossed the room and settled in to start signing.

"Don't listen to her," Brinn said, finally giving him a smile. "She's just a troublemaker."

"You know it!" Miranda called from across the room.

Brinn rolled her eyes and shook her head. "See?"

"I do." He walked over to the counter and leaned one hip against it as he glanced around the quiet store. "Looks like you're winding down for the day."

"Yeah. Only about forty-five minutes until closing time." She eyed him curiously. "Is there something I can help you with?"

"Yes. Dinner. Are you free?"

Her eyes widened for a second before she opened her mouth to speak and then closed it as if she wasn't quite sure what to say.

He took advantage of her moment of indecision. "How about The Cozy Cave for crab cakes? Are they still your favorite?"

Yes, but—"

"Perfect. I'll meet you back here at closing time, and we can walk over together."

"I meant yes they're still my favorite, but I haven't agreed to dinner."

"Yet," he added. "But we both know you can't pass up those crab cakes. I'm buying."

Brinn stared at him, but her resistance quickly vanished as

a smile claimed her pink lips. "It's not fair that you know my weaknesses."

He smirked. "Since you know mine, I'd say we're even. I'll be back in…" He glanced at his watch. "In exactly forty-two minutes."

"Just make sure you bring enough cash, cause I'm pretty sure I'm going to need a few margaritas to go with those crab cakes," Brinn called after him.

He turned just as he was ready to walk out the door. "Don't worry about that. There'll be enough for margaritas *and* flourless chocolate cake."

Right on cue, her cheeks flushed bright pink again. Austin winked at her, knowing neither of them would ever forget the night they'd celebrated her birthday with that flourless chocolate cake… naked.

As the door closed behind him, he heard Miranda's low whistle and couldn't help but feel pleased with himself.

Forty-two minutes later, Austin was back at Hollow Books with a bouquet of white lilies in one hand and a gift bag from Charming Herbals in the other.

He was just about to walk in when Brinn pulled the door open and said, "Maybe I should just…" She trailed off as her gaze landed on the flowers and then the bag.

"Maybe you should just what?" he asked, handing her the flowers.

Moisture glimmered in her eyes as she closed them briefly and brought the flowers up to her nose. Shaking her head, she said, "Nothing. Thank you. These are very thoughtful."

"You're welcome. I also saw this in the window display and thought of you." He handed her the bag from Charming Herbals.

Brinn took the bag tentatively and peeked in. When she

raised her gaze to Austin's, she narrowed her eyes at him suspiciously. "You just happened to see this in the window?"

He shrugged one shoulder. "Something like that."

"That's what I thought. Bree doesn't even stock this serum. It's made to order because it's so labor-intensive. How did you manage to just walk in and get a bottle?"

"Who said I just walked in?" he asked with a self-satisfied grin. The serum was a magical cream that Brinn had fallen in love with years ago for both the light lily scent and the fact that it did magical things for sensitive skin. She'd used it for as long as he'd known her, albeit sparingly because of its platinum price tag.

"You're saying you ordered this weeks ago?" she asked, sounding surprised.

Austin just smiled. "Ready for dinner?"

Her expression turned soft and tender as she nodded.

He slipped his hand into her free one, and when she didn't pull away, he let out a tiny contented sigh. He'd waited five long years for this moment. To move past her defenses and for her to let him back in. Austin knew he probably didn't deserve it, but he was grateful anyway.

"So about that flourless chocolate cake…" she said with a glint in her eye.

Austin nearly growled but managed to hold it back. "Are you suggesting—"

"No!" She shook her head and let out a bark of laughter. "I was going to say that they took it off the menu, so I guess you're out of luck."

"They did what?" Austin asked as he stopped dead in his tracks. "You're joking, right?"

"Afraid not," she said cheerfully. "The flourless chocolate cake will just have to live on in our memories."

"So wrong," Austin said, feigning disappointment. The fact that Brinn was flirting with him made him come alive. He'd do just about anything to keep her talking. "What about crème brûlée?"

"Not my favorite."

"Tiramisu?" he tried.

"I don't really want to think about eating anything that has ladyfingers in it. That's just... wrong."

He snorted. "How about homemade ice cream? Imagine what my tongue—"

"Okay, that's enough," she said, laughing. "I'm thinking there won't be room for dessert tonight."

"Just tonight? So you're saying we might indulge another time?"

"I'm not saying anything."

Her cheeks were flushing again, and it was all Austin could do to not pin her up against the building and kiss her right there. But now wasn't the time. He knew that if he pushed things past their harmless flirting right then, he'd ruin whatever was happening between them. Brinn needed time, and he wasn't going to do anything to mess up this chance she seemed to be giving him.

"Fair enough," he agreed. "But I like that the door appears to be open."

"You're relentless." She rolled her eyes, but the curve of her lips told him another story.

"Just hopeful." He squeezed her hand lightly, knowing that the magic they'd shared was still right there between them, sparking just as brightly as it had before. He knew then that if she opened the door to her heart, he'd never be able to leave her again.

"Oh no!" Brinn said suddenly.

"What is it?" But as soon as the words left his mouth, he spotted the problem. They were standing in front of the Cozy Cave, and there was a sign on the door indicating they were closed for a family emergency. "Damn." He glanced across at Woodlines, the packed restaurant across the street. "We could see how long it will take to get a table."

Brinn frowned. "Looks like a long wait. There are people three deep on the sidewalk and I'm starving. Maybe we should just take a rain check."

Austin shook his head. He was not throwing in the towel so easily. "I have a better idea."

"Yeah, what's that?"

"Come over to my house. I'll cook," he said.

"You cook?" she asked, sounding skeptical. "Since when?"

"Since I couldn't find decent crab cakes in LA. It took a bit of convincing, but I managed to get the Cozy Cave's recipe. Are you interested?"

"You know how to make their crab cakes?" She jerked a thumb in the direction of the restaurant.

"I've made them before, yes."

"Let's go." Brinn grabbed his hand and started tugging him back down the street.

Austin smiled to himself and gladly followed.

CHAPTER 8

*A*fter a quick trip to the grocery store, Brinn followed Austin into his grandmother's house. She'd been there before when they'd dated, but it was different now. Less cluttered and more masculine. The first thing she noticed was that the floral curtains Peggy had made had been taken down, leaving only the plain white wooden blinds. Most of Peggy's knickknacks had been removed as well. Brinn had to admit she liked the changes, but it made her sad, too, as the realization that she'd never see Peggy again hit her hard.

Tears filled her eyes, but she blinked them back. Austin didn't need her crying over his grandmother. He had his own grief to deal with. When they entered the kitchen, the clicking of dog nails on the tiles was quickly followed by a yip and a whine as Oz, Austin's puppy, ran toward them, his tail wagging in excitement.

"Yeah, buddy," Austin said, reaching down to pick him up. "I have a surprise for you."

Brinn's heart squeezed as she immediately reached out to take him.

Oz squirmed, nearly wiggling his way out of Austin's grip as he desperately tried to get to Brinn. She caught him as he jumped into her arms and licked furiously at her face, making whimpering noises the entire time.

"Dang, Oz. Way to cut in on my action," Austin said.

"He's not cutting in on anything," Brinn said, snuggling the pup. "We have five years of kisses and snuggles to catch up on."

Austin grunted, but there was a smile on his face as he moved to the counter to unload his groceries.

Brinn took her time loving on Oz until the white and gold Lhasa Apso wiggled to get down. When she finally set him on his feet, she patted his head and said, "I sure did miss you, boy."

He turned and licked her hand before running off to get water.

Brinn wiped at her eyes and then glanced around the kitchen. "What happened to the chicken canisters?"

Austin set a vase filled with water on the counter. "They're in storage with all the other kitschy stuff my grandmother never could resist."

"Okay, I hear you," Brinn said with a chuckle as she settled the lilies into the vase. "But you have to admit that the chickens were pretty good. Especially the one that was mooning everyone."

"They aren't really my aesthetic," Austin said and moved the lilies to the dining room table that was adjacent to the kitchen.

"Oh, come on. That's hardly the point. They were funny because your grandma always giggled when someone mentioned them. The memory alone is worth keeping them out."

"Would you leave them in your kitchen if you were trying to declutter a house full of forty years of stuff?" he asked.

"The chickens? Absolutely. But not the salt and pepper

collection or the cow-themed chip bowl. Whoever decided to put udders on a chip and dip bowl was seriously disturbed."

Austin laughed as he reached for a wine bottle from the wine rack. "I couldn't agree more." He held the bottle up. "Care for a glass?"

"Yes, please." Brinn settled on a bar stool at the kitchen island and watched as he poured them both a glass.

Austin held his glass up. "A toast? To… crab cakes and good wine."

Brinn touched her glass to his as she echoed his words, hating that they felt so… safe. In a perfect world, they'd be toasting to a new beginning. But that was a road she couldn't go down, and he knew that.

"Why are you frowning?" Austin asked, opening a container of crab meat.

"I'm not frowning," she insisted as she pasted a smile on her face.

"If you say so," he said with a smirk.

Brinn smirked back and took a long sip of her wine.

As Austin busied himself working on their dinner, Brinn was surprised to see him move around the kitchen with ease. When they'd been dating, he'd barely known how to boil water. "How and when did you learn how to cook?"

"Surprised?" he asked, a glint of mischief in his gaze.

"Yes. I figured you'd either live on take out or frozen pizza."

He feigned mock hurt as he grabbed his heart. "You wound me. Frozen pizza? Never."

"Uh-huh. I bet you have some in your freezer right now," she teased.

He cut his gaze to the freezer and said, "What's the bet?"

Brinn shook her head. "That was hyperbole. We don't need to actually bet."

"Nope. You put down the challenge. Name your terms," he said with a grin.

Oh, there was no way she could back down now. This had been a thing with them, always betting on little things. Only their terms had once been of a more... intimate nature. She felt her face flush again, and nearly scowled when Austin's grin widened. "Stop it."

"Stop what?" he asked innocently.

"You know what. You're amused that I keep blushing. Just stop."

"Being amused?"

"Yes! That."

He chuckled. "I'm not sure that's something I can promise. Now, about that bet..."

"Fine." She rolled her eyes, but couldn't help the huff of laughter that escaped her lips. "If there's a pizza in that freezer, you owe me a ninety-minute massage. If there isn't, I owe you a balloon ride in Napa Valley."

"Wow. You're going all out, aren't you? Balloon ride? You sure you're up for that?" he asked. "What about the spirits that might be roaming around?"

"Ghosts probably aren't hanging around at two thousand feet, but that's hardly the point. Who said I was going with you?" she asked. "I was just going to buy you a ticket and send you on your way."

"*Tickets*," he stressed. "Whatever I win, I want you to join me, so make sure you're up for it. Are you sure you don't want to change the terms?"

"Nope. The terms are fine," she said, waving a dismissive hand. "I know you've always wanted to go, and if you insist on having me there, I can just cross it off my bucket list."

"You have a bucket list?" he asked, sounding surprised.

"Of course I do. Doesn't everyone?"

"I doubt it, but I like this development. Tell me what else is on it, and I'll start making plans."

Brinn shook her head. "One activity at a time, Steele. Got it?"

"Fine," he said in mock irritation. "The terms are set, but I do think it's only fair that since you'll be joining me if I win, then I should get to participate if *you* win."

"What do you mean—" She stopped talking abruptly when she realized that he thought he'd be the one giving her a massage. Her entire body tingled with anticipation. Memories flooded her mind, sending a shiver up her spine. No. She needed to stop that line of thinking. "Um, when I said a ninety-minute massage, I meant a session at A Touch of Magic. Just to be clear."

"Ah, I see." Austin took another sip of his wine. "I'm glad we cleared that up. But still, if you win, I'll book a couples massage. It only seems appropriate."

Brinn eyed him. "I think this means you definitely have a frozen pizza in that freezer."

He raised both hands palms up. "To be honest, I'm not really sure. I sometimes do get them for convenience, but I can't remember if I've purchased any since I've been here." He walked over to the freezer. "Ready to see what it's going to be? Massages or a balloon ride?"

"You're incorrigible. You know that, right?"

"It's better than boring." He pulled the door open and gestured for her to take a look.

Brinn scanned the freezer but didn't see anything in a box. No pizza nor any frozen meals at all. It looked like she was taking a trip to Napa to fly around in a hot air balloon... alone with her ex. Holy crow, what had she gotten herself into? The only things the freezer held were cuts of different kinds of meat and fish as well as some frozen fruits and vegetables. "What, no ice cream either?"

"Check behind the frozen fruit," he said.

"Tell me you have chocolate caramel delight. The kind that has literal ribbons of caramel running through it." Brinn's mouth watered just thinking about the decadent dessert.

"There's only one way to find out." Austin went back to the island to start working on dinner again while Brinn scouted his freezer.

Once the fruit was pushed aside, Brinn leaned down and eyed the small appliance sitting in the back. "That's... Oh. Em. Gee." She spun around to face him. "You have an ice cream maker?"

"Looks like it, doesn't it?" he said, obviously pleased with himself. "I might even have ingredients for chocolate caramel."

"I think I'm in love," she said and then quickly slapped her hand over her mouth.

Austin met her gaze, his smile gone and an almost pained expression on his face.

"Sorry," she said softly.

"Don't apologize. I just hope one day you'll say that again and mean it."

His words shocked her into silence. Then frustration took over, and she moved in, crowding his space. "Austin?"

"Yes?" he asked, staring down at her.

"That's not something you get to say to me. Not here. Not now."

"Why not? It's the truth," he said.

"Because I'm not going there with you. We can try to be friends. Share a meal. Remember your grandmother. But to pretend we're ever going to be anything more, it's just not something we should do." She glanced around then, wishing things were different. That he hadn't left town. That he hadn't felt as though he didn't have a choice. And most importantly, that he had trusted her enough to tell her his plans. She forced herself to look at him again. "I don't want to talk about that. It's too hard."

He took a moment to process her words and then nodded slowly. "Understood. My apologies." There wasn't any hint of his amusement or teasing from earlier. Serious Austin had replaced the easygoing man she'd fallen in love with all those years ago. And dammit if that didn't make her want to take back her words. Tell him that she wanted to hear him tell her he loved her. That he wanted to stay right there in Keating Hollow with her... forever. Her stomach fluttered as if that were an actual possibility.

It wasn't.

Brinn knew he had a successful business to get back to. Even if he wanted to stay, he couldn't. Not when he had people counting on him.

When Brinn turned her attention back to Austin, he was busy placing the crab cakes in the pan to fry them. A sauce that looked exactly like the one the Cozy Cave served was already made and sitting off to the side. When had he made that? Had she been so caught up in her own head that she hadn't even noticed? It appeared so.

"I can help with the ice cream while you finish those," Brinn said, trying to push her thoughts of a reconciliation with Austin out of her mind. She'd have better luck if she stayed busy.

"If you're up for it, sure," he said. "The recipe is in that first drawer."

Brinn dug it out, and after reading it over, she nodded and

got to work. Fifteen minutes later, just as Austin was plating their crab cakes, Brinn turned the ice cream maker on and set a timer. "It needs to set up, and then I can put the caramel in it."

Austin peered in the machine and nodded. "Looks good. Let's eat before these get cold."

Brinn followed him over to the table where Oz was already waiting for them. There were two place settings with his grandmother's favorite China and flatware. "It's almost like she's still here."

Just as she spoke, one of the kitchen windows popped open and wind whistled through the room.

She and Austin stared at each other and then as if on cue, they both started laughing.

"Well, that was unexpected," Brinn said, jumping up to close the window.

But Austin beat her too it. "I wouldn't read too much into it. I've been meaning to replace this latch ever since I got back in town. Sometimes it doesn't catch correctly."

"Sure. Likely story." It was her turn to tease.

Austin gave her a half smile as he closed and locked the window. Then he leaned against the counter with his arms crossed over his chest. "Though it wouldn't bother me if she was here."

"No?" It would bother Brinn. While she'd love the chance to say goodbye to Peggy, one just never knew how a ghost would react to their own death. She didn't want to deal with a distraught spirit who wasn't quite in her right mind. Brinn had loved Peggy and had often thought of her as a surrogate grandmother. Peggy Steele had been one of very few adults who'd watched out for Brinn over the years, and Brinn missed her. She didn't want to tarnish that memory if she could help it.

"Let's just say that I have a few questions. Ones that should have been answered long before I dealt with her trust," Austin said, sounding tired.

Brinn took her seat at the table again, giving Austin her undivided attention. "What is it? What's wrong?"

Austin let out a long breath as he ran a hand over his short hair. "Ah, it's nothing really. Just a detail with her trust that doesn't make any sense."

"What detail?" Brinn pressed. It was clear there was something that was weighing on Austin, and she wanted to help. "I don't know if you know this, but I stayed good friends with your grandmother after you left."

"She mentioned that you two got together every now and then," Austin said.

Brinn snorted. "Every now and then? More like twice a week, every week. We had standing dates to meet for coffee and pedicures. She told me things. Maybe I can help."

"She didn't tell you this," he said with a sigh.

"Try me."

"It has to do with Gideon Alexander. Any idea why she'd leave him a small fortune?" Austin asked. By his flat tone, she knew he didn't expect her to have answers.

"She left a small fortune to Gideon?" Brinn's eyes widened. There was a story there, but she'd be damned if she could figure it out.

"Yep," Austin confirmed. "Even Gideon claims he has no idea why."

"That's… Well, it's incredible. It's not like he needs the money," Brinn said, almost to herself. "Looks like he's doing just fine. Right?"

Austin nodded and groaned when the window popped

open again. "Grandma," he said, "if that's you, you have stop this."

The wind immediately died down, and Austin turned to Brinn. "You saw that, right?"

She nodded, clutching her hands to her midsection.

"You have to talk to her," Austin said, urgency in his tone.

"I... I don't do that anymore," she said. "You know that."

"Brinn, please. This is my grandmother. I need to know if she was manipulated before I hand off a very large check."

Brinn stood, saw the expectation in his eyes, and shook her head. "No. Is that why you brought me here? Thinking I'd see her and then you could use me as a medium?" Like everyone else at college had when they'd learned of her ability.

"What? No, I—"

"Forget it," Brinn said, her jaw clenched. "I should be used to it by now."

"Used to what?" he asked as he followed her to the door. "What did I do?"

"You ruined it," Brinn said sadly. "I don't talk to ghosts anymore."

Austin nodded. "I just thought that while she was here, you'd want to talk to her."

"She's here?"

The world spun slightly, and suddenly Brinn found herself face-to-face with the ghost of Peggy Steele.

"Hello, dear," Peggy said. "Are you ready? We have much to discuss."

Brinn sucked in a sharp breath, glared at Austin, and then said, "I can't do this. I can't open that door again. " With panic flooding her veins, Brinn grabbed her coat and made a beeline for the door, leaving Austin and Oz behind... with a delicious plate of crab cakes.

"Brinn wait!" Austin called.

But she didn't look back. She couldn't for fear that Peggy would be right behind her. What else did ghosts have to do?

Bother Brinn, that's what. She gritted her teeth and made a note to order more sage. When she got home, she went straight to bed, trying to convince herself that the date hadn't been a setup to get her to communicate with Peggy.

But something deep inside of her said that it had been. And she'd learned long ago to trust her gut. And that meant she couldn't trust Austin Steele.

CHAPTER 9

*B*rinn sat at the end of her couch, scratching Buffy's ears and staring at the untouched tuna sandwich. The sad, no mayo tuna sandwich she'd thrown together because her fridge was almost empty and she'd run out on Austin before she'd had a chance to eat her dinner. And dammit, those crab cakes had looked and smelled amazing. Why had he insisted she needed to talk to his dead grandmother before she'd eaten?

Why had he insisted at all? Austin knew how she felt about communicating with the dead. Besides, there wasn't anything they could learn from her that would change the trust documents, so Brinn just didn't see the point.

She closed her eyes, and the image of her own grandmother standing in the bookstore flashed in her mind. Brinn had been momentarily stunned, but then had reached out to her, desperate to talk to her again. But as soon as Brinn opened her mouth, her grandmother had vanished. As much as Brinn didn't want to talk to spirits, she'd been happy to see her grandmother.

Afterward, the anxiety had set in.

Why had she seen her grandmother? She was the second ghost that had appeared to her in Keating Hollow in less than a week. Would she start seeing them everywhere now?

That question, more than anything, was what had sent her running from Austin's house. If spirits started bothering her in Keating Hollow, what would she do then?

Buffy put her paw on Brinn's hand as if the pure white cat knew she needed comfort.

"Thanks, Buffy," Brinn murmured and leaned down to kiss her kitty on the head. "What should we do about this spirit thing?"

Buffy looked up at Brinn, her green eyes bright.

"Yeah, I don't know either."

THE FAINT GLOW of the computer lit Brinn's bedroom. She was sitting up in bed, searching for any information on mediums in the area. So far, she hadn't found any within a hundred-mile radius. Not any that looked legit or advertised, anyway.

Brinn rubbed at her gritty eyes. She'd barely gotten a few hours of sleep. All she kept seeing were flashes of her grandmother and the look on Austin's face when he'd wanted her to talk to Peggy.

If spirits had found her in Keating Hollow, she was going to need to learn how to block them out. She could not live like she did when she was in college. She'd lose her mind.

Without any mediums to consult, she decided she'd try the next best thing.

Forty minutes later, Brinn was dressed and had a thermal mug in hand as she left her house. The sun was shining, trying its best to burn off the morning fog. She steered her Prius toward the center of town, determined to get some answers.

Brinn parked in front of Charming Herbals and peered at the closed sign on the front door. She sat back, drinking her coffee, and waited. And waited some more.

Finally, the sign was turned, and Brinn hurried into the shop.

"Good morning, Brinn." Bree Burgess smiled warmly at her. "What can I do for you today?"

"I need a serum," Brinn blurted. "It's an emergency."

"The skin serum?" She frowned and her brows pinched together. "I don't have any in stock. You didn't order any, recently did you?"

"Oh no. That's not... I'm here for something else. It's pretty obscure, but I'm hoping you can help or at least point me in the right direction."

"Okay." Bree moved behind the counter and glanced at the shelves behind her. "What is it I'm looking for?"

"Spirit repellant."

Bree blinked at her. "Did you say spirit repellant?"

"Yes."

"Like a bug spray you use before venturing into the woods?" Bree's lips twitched, but she managed to keep the smile at bay.

"Yes, exactly like that. I need something that will keep ghosts from bothering me. Do you have something like that? A spray? A potion? A spell?"

Bree stepped back out from behind the counter and led Brinn over to a set of chairs near the window. After taking a seat, she turned to Brinn and said, "Do you want to tell me what's going on? Do you have a ghost that suddenly turned up in your house? Because you know that sage will—"

"I have sage," Brinn said, shaking her head. "I don't have one living in my house, at least I don't think I do. My grandmother might be hanging around sometimes, but I wouldn't need sage for her."

"Okay, then I don't understand. What's the issue?"

Brinn took a deep breath and let it out slowly. Then she met the other woman's concerned green eyes. "I don't talk about this... ever. There are only a couple of people who even know about it, so if you wouldn't mind keeping this to yourself, I'd appreciate it."

"Okay. Sure." Bree frowned, obviously trying to make sense of where Brinn was going with this.

"I'm a medium," Brinn blurted.

Bree's eyes widened. "Really? Wow. That's... wow," she said again. "I've never met a medium before. It's a pretty rare gift, isn't it?"

"It appears so, but I'd hardly call it a gift," Brinn said with a huff of irritation. "You have no idea what it's like to be followed around and harassed by a spirit who just wants revenge on her cheating husband."

"Oh, dear. Is that happening now?" Bree craned her neck as she peered around Brinn as if looking for the ghost in question.

"No. But it has happened in the past."

"How often?" Bree asked.

Brinn slumped into the chair. "When I was away at college, I saw ghosts all the time. Daily. The crazy ones were more like once every couple of weeks. But here in Keating Hollow, I never see them. Or at least I never used to, but I've seen two this week and a possible third. I just can't go back to being inundated like that again. Surely there must be something that can be done to ward them off."

"That sounds very... disruptive."

"You could say that." Brinn stood and started to pace the store. "Do you have any suggestions?"

Bree bit her bottom lip and then grimaced. "I'm sorry to say that I don't. This isn't something anyone has asked for before. Since the gift, or curse as you might see it, is so rare, it's unlikely any of my suppliers have anything either. But I can certainly look into it for you."

"You will?" Brinn felt a twinge of hope as she stared at the herbalist. "Will you call me if you find anything? Anything at all?"

"I will." Bree gave her a reassuring smile. "I'll do my best. The moment I have any information for you, I'll get in touch."

"Thank you." Brinn gave the other woman a hug, grateful to have someone who was willing to try to help her with her new problem.

Bree hugged her back awkwardly and then let out a nervous chuckle. "I haven't done anything yet."

"But you will," Brinn said definitively. There was no room for doubt. Not for her. She knew what it was like to live with no peace. She couldn't do it again.

"I will try," Bree promised.

"That's all I can ask for." Brinn thanked her for her help and then walked back outside. What was she supposed to do now? Charming Herbals was the only place she could think to go for help. She scanned Main Street, hoping that a psychic or tarot reader had opened up shop.

No such luck.

Brinn got in her car, intending to head back home, but when she spotted a familiar car out in front of the Keating Hollow Brewery, she spontaneously made a detour and parked next to Abby Townsend's new red Honda SUV.

It was still early in the day, but despite the closed sign, the front door was open. Brinn peeked inside and found Abby sitting at the bar with a cup of coffee and a pastry from Incantation Café.

"Good morning, Brinn," Clay Garrison said.

Brinn glanced over and spotted Abby's husband striding toward her. He had a clipboard in his hand and a pen tucked behind one ear. "Hi, Clay. I know you're not open yet, but I was hoping to talk to Abby for a minute. Is it okay if I sit at the bar with her?"

"Of course, it is," Abby called from her spot. Her long blond hair was piled up into a messy bun, and she was wearing yoga pants and a sweatshirt as if she'd just rolled out of bed and headed to the brewery.

Clay's lips quirked. "The boss has spoken. Come on in."

"Thanks." Brinn weaved her way through the tables until she got to the bar and sat next to her cousin's best friend. "Morning."

"Morning," Abby said, flashing her a welcoming smile. "What brings you here so early?"

"You," Brinn said and pressed a hand to her forehead.

"Uh-oh. What's wrong?" Abby's expression turned concerned. "Is it Wanda? Did something happen?"

"No, no. Nothing like that," Brinn reassured her. "It's... me. I have an issue and could use a sounding board."

"Okay, shoot." She held up her pastry bag. "Coffee cake? I have an extra."

"Sure." Brinn took the coffee cake and was grateful for something else to focus on for a moment. She had no idea why she was sitting in the brewery with Abby. It wasn't like the other witch was a medium. She made soaps and potions and energy boosters. Still, she wasn't sure who else she could talk to.

"Clay," Abby called. "Do we have any fresh coffee? I think Brinn could use a jolt of caffeine."

"Is it that obvious? I barely slept last night."

"You just look a little pale. Nothing a nap won't fix," Abby offered.

Brinn snorted. "How diplomatic of you. But yes, I see a nap in my future if I can ever figure out how to relax again."

"What's keeping you up?" Abby asked.

"Ghosts."

"Seriously?" Abby asked, sounding far too excited by Brinn's answer.

"Yes, but they aren't keeping me up literally. There aren't any hanging out at my house. At least not any that I'm aware of. But I have seen a few around town, and I'm afraid I'm going to start seeing them all the time." She went on to explain how she learned she was a medium while she was in college, and the reason she moved back to Keating Hollow. "I don't want to see ghosts, so I need to figure out how to control this. I know you spent a lot of time in New Orleans. Did you ever see any?"

"Yes. A few times actually," she said, nodding. "But none of them spoke to me. They were just sort of an outline, hanging around in places they'd lived over a hundred years ago."

"That would be perfectly fine with me. Unfortunately, the ones I see want to talk," Brinn said and thanked Clay as he set a mug of coffee in front of her.

"That sounds kind of interesting," Abby said.

"Actually, it's invasive and overtakes my entire life. I don't want this." She turned to meet Abby's gaze. "I know this is a longshot, but have you ever heard of a potion or spell or something to keep spirits away?"

"Sure. I'd have to get in touch with a friend of mine from

New Orleans, but I'm pretty sure there's something other than just sage that protects people from spirits."

"Seriously?" Brinn pressed a hand to her chest as her heart began to beat wildly with anticipation.

"Seriously. Give me a day or two to make some calls, and I'll let you know what I find out."

"Abby," Brinn said. "If you weren't married, I'd kiss you right on the mouth. Thank you."

The other woman chuckled. "Don't get too excited. I don't have anything yet."

"But you're trying, and that's what matters right now. Thank you, thank you, thank you."

She chuckled. "You're welcome. I just hope I find something that works for you."

"I hope so, too."

Brinn stayed with Abby for a while and taste-tested a few of the new ciders the brewery had introduced over the holidays. Her favorite was the ginger flavor. It had just the right bite for a cold winter day.

By the time Brinn walked back into her house, she was smiling and full of hope that Abby would help her find a solution. Her three cats came running when they heard the door shut, and she laughed at them as they herded her toward the treat jar.

"Okay, okay. Settle down." She shook the bag of treats and watched as they tried to push each other out of the way. With the treats in her palm, she said, "You're supposed to be besties. That means being nice to each other."

Willow immediately sat, waiting patiently, while Buffy swatted Xander with her tail one last time.

Brinn couldn't help but laugh as she doled out the treats.

"Dang, Buf. I'm gonna start calling you Buffy the Cat Slayer. Not very nice of you."

Buffy just purred and rubbed herself along Brinn's leg.

"You're beyond shame, aren't you?"

Buffy moved between Brinn's legs and slinked off to the cat tree, where she perched on Xander's favorite section. Cleary the cat wasn't done torturing her brother.

Brinn picked up Xander and loved on him a bit. Just as she was putting him down, she caught a flash of movement in her living room. Frowning, she moved quickly to see who was there. But when she got to the doorway, she froze.

"Hello, Brinn," her grandmother said from her favorite spot near the fireplace.

"Grandma?" Brinn croaked. After she cleared her throat, she asked, "What... I mean why are you here?"

"To help you, of course."

"Help me to what?" Brinn asked, her voice was stronger now, but her entire body had broken out in gooseflesh. Whatever the reason for her grandmother's visit, she instantly knew it was important.

"To embrace your gift, sweetie. It's time."

Brinn's mouth went dry. "Why?"

"Because you have work to do." Her tiny grandmother gave her a reassuring smile and then vanished into the ether.

CHAPTER 10

*a*ustin walked into the Incantation Café and glanced around at the patrons, looking for Gideon Alexander. The place was crowded, with every table taken and a line almost to the door. It had been three days since he'd met with Gideon. Three days since he'd informed the man that he was getting a significant inheritance. Austin hadn't heard anything from him until two hours ago when the man had called and asked if they could meet.

"Hey, Austin. Over here," Miranda Moon called from across the café. She was sitting by a window, the sun shining on her dark hair.

He strode over, and when Miranda gestured for him to sit, he sat across from her.

Miranda had her phone out and was tapping on the screen. "What would you like? Gideon is already in line."

Austin craned his neck and spotted the other man. He was next in line. "Just a plain black coffee."

"Just coffee? Nah. You need a coffee cake or something, too." She tapped quickly.

"That's not—"

"Shhh!" She ordered and finished her text. Once she put the phone down on the table, she leaned forward and said, "I told him to get a variety of pastries. I was up late writing. Sugar is the only cure."

"The only one?" Austin asked, amused.

"And caffeine of course."

"Caffeine goes without saying," Austin agreed.

"You're a man after my own heart." Miranda continued to chatter on about writing and books until her fiancé appeared.

"Coffee's ready." Gideon placed the paper cups on the table and then arranged the variety of pastries on a paper plate.

Austin sat back in his chair, studying the couple. Gideon hadn't told him exactly why he wanted to meet. He'd just said he wanted to go over the inheritance situation. Austin thought the paperwork he'd left with Gideon had been fairly clear. If Gideon had questions, they likely could've been answered over the phone.

Unless Gideon wanted to contest it for some reason. But if that were the case, why were the pair of them so cheerful? He'd be unsuccessful anyway. The trust was pretty cut and dried.

Austin cleared his throat. "I don't mean to be rude, but can one of you tell me why we're meeting?"

Gideon and Miranda shared a quick glance before they both turned to look at him again. Gideon took a sip of his coffee, and when he placed the cup back on the table, he said, "I've spent the last three days thinking about this inheritance, and I think it's best if I decline. I barely knew your grandmother, and it doesn't seem right that I'd get what should be yours."

Stunned, Austin blinked at him. "That is not what I was expecting to hear."

"Really? What were you expecting?" Gideon asked, frowning at the other man.

"I really have no idea. I just didn't expect you to turn down a windfall of money. No one really does that, do they?"

Gideon let out a soft chuckle. "I'd guess not."

Miranda leaned in, lowering her voice. "Just between us, he doesn't need it. Didn't you hear? He has a sugar mama now."

The pair of them laughed at the obvious inside joke.

"Uh, okay," Austin said. "Well, I'm not sure what to say about this. I just want to honor my grandmother's wishes."

The laughter died out and Gideon's expression turned serious. "Listen. I completely understand that point of view. But I barely knew her. It doesn't seem right that I take that money."

"That's... noble of you," Austin said, still not settled on the idea. He'd been close to his grandmother. She hadn't been senile or confused when she'd passed. Since it seemed abundantly clear that Gideon hadn't orchestrated the change in the trust, Austin had to assume she had her reasons. And he wanted to honor them.

"It's just the right thing to do," Gideon said.

Austin shook his head. "I'm not sure it is, to be honest." He placed his hands flat on the table and leaned back in his chair. "Peggy Steele was a lot of things, but impulsive wasn't one of them. She was a very deliberate woman. If she left you this, it's because she had her reasons. The only part I'm unclear about is why she didn't tell me or leave some sort of explanation."

Gideon leaned back as well and let out a breath. "I honestly have no idea."

"Me neither," Miranda added.

"Were you close to my grandmother?" Austin asked,

peering at her more closely. Was it possible she had anything to do with this?

"Oh, no. Not at all. We'd met a few times in passing, and I liked her, but we were acquaintances at best. I tend to just know things sometimes." She gave him a soft smile. "It's one of my strange quirks."

She just knew things? Austin wondered what *things* she knew about him.

Miranda chuckled and slid her hand over Gideon's.

Gideon picked up a cheese pastry and took a bite. After he swallowed, he grinned. "Damn that's good."

Austin was getting restless. It wasn't that he didn't like the couple. He did. They seemed like really nice people. He just couldn't honor Gideon's request. "I appreciate what you're trying to do, Gideon. I really do. But I can't go against my grandmother's wishes. I had the utmost respect for her. If she wanted to give you part of her estate, then that's what we should do. No doubt she had her reasons."

Gideon shook his head in bewilderment as he stared at Austin for a moment. "I just don't understand it."

"That makes two of us," Austin said honestly. "We were pretty close. It's really strange to me that she didn't tell me about it or leave some sort of explanation. But that's beside the point. I don't have to know her reasons. I have her trust and that's enough. If you don't want to keep the money, then find a charity or do something else good with it. It's your choice."

The other man's expression suddenly turned thoughtful. "Giving it to a charity is a good idea."

"How about the Artist in Residence program?" Miranda asked. "Seems like a no-brainer since you're involved already."

"You are?" Austin asked.

Gideon nodded. "The artist will get to show their work in

my gallery. I'll also be mentoring the business side of selling art."

"Does the program pay you for that?" Austin asked, very curious about how the program worked.

"Nope," Gideon said easily. "My time and the art space are donated. The funds the town council are raising are for lodging and stipends."

"That's really cool." Austin had already liked the man sitting across from him, but now he respected him, too. He wondered if his grandmother had witnessed his generosity as well.

"It really is, isn't it?" Miranda said, smiling softly at her fiancé.

Gideon slipped his hand over Miranda's and squeezed.

The gesture was minor, yet Austin felt a surge of jealousy. He wanted what they had. The type of relationship where partners support each other and are nauseatingly happy. He'd had that once with Brinn. If he hadn't walked away— No, there was no point in trying to change the past. What was done was done. He just had to hope that there was room for a second chance.

"What do you think about a kids art program? One that could be run year-round?" Gideon asked.

Austin felt a cool rush of air wash over him, followed by the hair standing up on his arms. And he just knew in that moment that his grandmother Peggy loved that idea. "It's perfect. Exactly the sort of thing my grandmother would be excited about."

Gideon sat back and smiled easily at Austin. "Perfect. It's settled then. I'll work on setting up a kid's non-profit for the arts."

"What if I said I would like to be a part of it?" Austin asked.

"Oh… Well, it is your grandmother's money. I suppose you should have a say," Gideon said.

"No. You misunderstand what I'm trying to say." Austin took a sip of his coffee and then continued. "I want to combine my share of the inheritance to the new foundation. And add a music program."

Gideon leaned forward, staring Austin in the eye. "You're serious, aren't you?"

"As serious as it gets," Austin said. "If you're willing to work with me, then I want in. I can't think of a better way to honor my grandmother than this."

"Okay. You're on." Gideon held his hand out to Austin.

Austin took it, grasping on tightly. "To our new partnership."

"To our new partnership," he echoed.

Miranda grinned at both of them. "Well, isn't this exciting?"

"I'd say so," Gideon agreed. "What do you think, Miranda? Are we destined for greatness?"

She glanced at both of them, and then her gaze turned unfocused as she stared at nothing. Slowly, her head bobbed up and down. "Yes. This union is destined for greatness."

Austin raised his eyebrows, not sure what to make of Miranda Moon and her strange prediction. "Uh, so is this part of that gift you have for *knowing things?*"

"It sure seems like it," Gideon said, his tone serious.

Miranda turned to him, her lips curved into a mischievous smile and her eyes laughing.

"You're just messing with me, aren't you?" Austin said, narrowing his eyes at her.

She shrugged. "Maybe. Maybe not. But now that I've put it out there into the universe, I wouldn't bet against it."

"Me neither," Gideon said as he pulled a pen out of his pocket and grabbed a napkin. "Ready to start making plans?"

Austin chuckled, knowing deep down all the way to his bones that he wasn't going to regret working with Gideon Alexander. He leaned forward, his elbows on the table, and said, "There's no time like the present."

CHAPTER 11

*B*rinn turned her back on the fiery redhead as she slid a stack of books on a shelf. If she just ignored the ghost, she knew from personal experience that she'd likely run out of energy and disappear for at least a few hours.

"I'm telling you, Bob was a jackhammer. He just climbed on top of me and started ramming away as if my hoo haw needed to be punished. That man *needs* my evaluation if he's ever going to keep a Kimmie around. And what about poor Kimmie? She doesn't deserve that treatment. Nor does she deserve to have her breasts tweaked like an old-fashioned radio. All Bob needs is a link to some high-quality nipple clamps and—"

"For the love of everything under the sun!" Brinn spun around, itching to strangle the ghost. "Stop talking right now. You're giving me a massive headache."

"You know what would really help that man? My evaluation. If he learned where the magic button—"

"No. No talk about magic buttons. Just no," Brinn said. "Go away. I have work to do."

The curvy redhead crossed her arms over her chest and narrowed her eyes at Brinn. "I'm trying to do the world a service. Take Timothy. When I gave him his evaluation, not only did he thank me, but he rewarded me by tossing me down on a table and—"

"Argh!" Brinn cried and clamped her hands over her ears. So much for ignoring the ghost until she ran out of energy.

"Brinn?" Yvette called as she rounded the corner. "What's wrong?"

Brinn sucked in a deep breath and let it out as she met her employer's worried eyes.

"Hey," Yvette asked gently. "Are you okay?"

"No, she isn't okay," the ghost said, sounding annoyed. "She's losing it. All I want is for someone to deliver my evaluations. My former partners deserve their feedback."

"You can't hear that, can you?" Brinn asked Yvette.

"Hear what?" she asked, frowning.

"That's what I thought." Brinn buried her face in her hands and let out a groan.

"You're kinda freaking me out," Yvette said.

"I know." Brinn walked away from the stack of books she'd been shelving and made her way to the bookstore's café. "I need sugar. You in?"

"I think I'd better." Yvette followed her to the café and sat at one of the tables while Brinn raided the pastry case.

The red-headed ghost slid up next to Brinn and whispered, "I'm not going away. Not until—" The ghost's eyes widened as her words were suddenly silenced. A second later, she vanished.

Brinn let out a long breath as she made a couple of mocha lattes. When she was done, she held up the whipped cream canister in a silent question to Yvette.

Yvette nodded and got up to grab the tray of cheese danishes and pumpkin scones.

"Here you go." Brinn handed Yvette her mocha latte with a mound of whipped cream taller than the cup.

"This is serious," Yvette teased before taking a mouthful of whipped cream.

Brinn followed her lead and then ate an entire pumpkin scone before she sat back in her chair, ready to talk about the problem that wasn't going away. "I'm seeing ghosts. All the time."

Yvette's eyes widened. "All the time?"

"Yep." She glanced past her boss, spotting another ghost making a beeline for her. This one was short and round with a neat bun on the top of her head, and she wore a blueberry-stained apron.

"Tell me everything about that scone. The flavor, the texture, the sweetness profile. Did it melt in your mouth?" the ghost demanded.

Brinn knew from experience that if she entertained the ghost, she'd leave faster. "Pumpkin. Just the perfect amount of moisture so it wasn't too dry. Mildly sweet. I think it was sweetened with maple syrup. And yes, it absolutely melted in my mouth."

"Uh, Brinn?" Yvette asked, her brows knit in confusion. "What…?"

"Tell me about the danish," the ghost said, staring longingly at the tray.

"A pastry chef ghost just showed up. She won't leave until I describe the cheese danish." Brin gave Yvette an exasperated whisper of a smile.

"Oh," Yvette said. She nodded and then picked up one of the cheese danishes. "I'll do it." She took a bite, closed her eyes, and savored the danish. After she swallowed, she opened her eyes and said, "Creamy cream cheese filling with just a hint of sweetness and a flaky dough drizzled with a light sugar glaze. It's like eating a cheese-filled cloud."

The ghost snorted. "Cheese-filled cloud? That one is terrible at this. But it'll do for now." The ghost waved at Brinn and walked back across the store, disappearing behind the wall.

"How did I do?" Yvette asked Brinn.

"Well enough that she was amused and left. However, she insinuated you should keep your day job."

Yvette chuckled. "Fair enough. There's a reason we get our bakery items from Incantation Café."

"It's good to know your strengths," Brinn said, slumping in her chair.

"Are you okay?" Yvette asked. "You sound exhausted."

"That's no surprise. I haven't gotten any sleep in four days," Brinn said, rubbing at her eyes. "The ghosts just started showing up all of a sudden, and I swear it's getting worse as time goes on."

"Was it this bad when you were away at college?"

Brinn shook her head. "No, but it was bad enough. I never knew when they'd show up or how persistent they'd be, but it wasn't this constant. I barely get a break before another one shows up."

As if right on cue, a third ghost appeared. The tall blonde with worried eyes stood right behind Yvette, her hands clutched together so tightly that her knuckles were turning white. "Please. You have to check on Henry. Make sure he went to his cardiologist. His heart is weak, and without me around to make sure he makes his appointments, I'm afraid he'll forget. Please. I want him to live a long, happy life even if mine was cut short."

Brinn nodded. "Sure. I'll check on Henry. Where do I find him?"

The ghost sighed in relief and then rattled off an address at the retirement village. "He just turned fifty-five. Seems unfair he has heart problems so soon."

"It does seem unfair," Brinn agreed.

"You're a godsend," the ghost said, smiling at Brinn. "I don't know how to thank you."

"No thanks necessary, but I do need to get back to work." Brinn stood abruptly, praying the ghost would leave her alone now that she'd agreed to do her bidding.

The ghost grinned and added, "I'll check back in the morning to see what you found out."

Brinn stood there silently fuming. While she was still waiting to find out if Bree or Abby had any information for her, she had all but given up hope that she'd ever have a normal life again. Keating Hollow was no longer her sanctuary. That much was clear.

Yvette cleared her throat.

Brinn met the other woman's eyes. "My life is a shit show. Can you imagine what this looks like to people who have no idea I'm being harassed by spirits?"

"It's rather disconcerting even to those of us who are aware," she said carefully. "I wish there was something I could do to help. That's got to be…"

"Torturous?" Brinn asked. Before Yvette could answer her, Brinn threw up her hands. "This is insane! How am I supposed to keep living like this? I can't sleep. I can barely eat. And now working is almost impossible!"

Yvette opened her mouth to say something, but then stopped abruptly and stared over Brinn's shoulder.

"Hello, Yvette," a familiar voice said.

Brinn spun and found her grandmother standing just behind her with a concerned look on her face. Brinn glanced at Yvette, back to her grandmother, and then to Yvette again. "Did you just hear her?"

Yvette nodded and turned her attention to Violet Taylor. "Hello, Violet. This is… a surprise."

"I imagine it is. You don't normally see ghosts, do you?"

Yvette shook her head. "I never have before. Do you know why I am now?" She had a worried expression as she glanced around the shop. "Am I going to start seeing them all the time now, too?"

"No, hun. You're only seeing me because of my magic." Violet turned to her granddaughter. "Are you okay?"

"No. I'm not okay at all," Brinn said, her voice catching on a sob lodged in her throat. The events of the past few days, combined with the fact that her grandmother was there speaking to her and Yvette as if she'd never died, it was all too much. Silent tears streamed down her face.

"Oh, Brinn." Yvette wrapped an arm around her shoulders and gave her a sideways hug.

"It's okay, baby girl," Violet said softly. "I'm here now."

Brinn stared at her grandmother. "You… said…" She sucked in a shaky breath. "You said I had work to do."

Violet stepped up and cupped her wrinkled hands against Brinn's cheeks, holding her gaze. "You do. But I'm here to tell you how to manage this gift."

"You are?" Brinn asked, feeling a sense of calm wash over her. It was the first time in days that she didn't feel like she wanted to crawl right out of her skin.

"I am." She nodded and grabbed both of Brinn's hands.

Brinn stared down at their joined hands, wondering how come she could feel her grandmother touching her. None of the other ghosts that visited her had been in solid form.

"It's because while I was alive, I was a spirit witch. The magic doesn't just go away," Violet explained as if she were reading Brinn's mind. She squeezed Brinn's hands. "That's what you are, too. A spirit witch. It's why you can see and talk to ghosts."

"What?" Brinn asked and then shook her head. "No, Grandma. I'm an air witch. Remember? Not a great one, but it's the one element I was able to manipulate."

Violet smiled patiently. "Why do you think you were never very good at animating objects?"

"Because I'm a mediocre witch?"

"No. It's because you're a spirit witch who has a small affinity for manipulating air."

Brinn frowned at her grandmother. "What do you mean?"

"Exactly what I said, sweet pea. You've always had this ability. But when you were younger, it was far too overwhelming for you. So I did what I could to shield you. When you went away for college, it was clear your gift was far more powerful than you could handle at the time, so when you came back, I shielded you again. Now my magic is fading, and it's time for you to learn to embrace it. Like I said before, there's work for you to do."

"But…" Brinn felt empty, as if everything she'd ever trusted had been ripped away. Her grandmother had kept this all a secret. She didn't understand. "Why didn't you tell me before?"

Violet placed a hand on Brinn's arm. "I just wanted to protect you. I meant to tell you before my heart attack. I just… Time got away from me. I always knew your ability would get stronger, that I couldn't protect you forever. Is it wrong that I wanted you to have as much time as possible before you had no choice in the matter?"

"No." Brinn stared at her grandmother, missing her with everything she had. "I wish you could stay with me. Help me through this. Can you, or will you disappear like the rest of them?"

Violet gave her a sad smile. "I have more energy than most, but I too will have to leave you for a while. But I can leave you with some advice."

"Okay." Brinn wiped her cheeks, hoping to put on a brave face for her grandmother.

"Austin's home is a safe space for you. There are ancient wards surrounding the property that make it so that most spirits can't bother you there. Go spend time with him. You'll get peace there."

"But last time I was there, we both thought we felt Peggy. Are you sure?" Brinn asked her.

"I'm sure. Peggy might be there, but she won't bother you." Violet's form was starting to flicker, indicating they only had a few moments left.

"I can't just show up at Austin's door," Brinn insisted.

"We both know that's not true. Go. Find your center before…" Violet faded away, her next words dying on her lips.

"Before what?" Brinn called.

Silence filled the bookstore.

"Grandma!" Brinn squeezed her eyes shut and shook her head. "I can't do this."

"Sure you can," Yvette said at the same time another voice chimed in with, "Whoa. That was intense."

Both Brinn and Yvette turned to see Hope Garber, Yvette's half sister, staring at them.

"I'm so sorry," Hope said, her pale face flushing red. "I didn't mean to intrude. I just walked in and there you were, talking to a ghost... I mean your grandmother, and I've never seen a ghost before. I just sort of froze. I should go." She spun around and headed back toward the front door.

"No!" Brinn and Yvette called at the same time. They glanced at each other, Yvette chuckling while Brinn gave her an apologetic smile.

"I'm sorry," Brinn whispered. "I don't want my drama scaring off anyone, especially one of your sisters."

Yvette squeezed her hand. "You're not." The bookstore owner turned to Hope. "Right, Hope?"

Hope glanced around, clearly checking to see if the shop was overrun with any more spirits, and then she moved back toward Yvette. "Sorry. I just kinda freaked a little there, didn't I?"

"A little. Who knew you'd be the skittish one?" Yvette teased.

Hope snorted. "Well, I've definitely seen a lot of things, going through foster care and all, but ghosts aren't one of them. You haven't ever mentioned the bookstore being haunted before."

"The whole town is haunted," Brinn said, sounding bitter to her own ears.

"Really?" Hope raised both eyebrows. "Even at the spa?"

Hope Garber was the half sister of the Townsend sisters. She'd been born after their mother had left their father, and they hadn't found each other until a couple years prior when Hope had settled in Keating Hollow and started working at A Touch of Magic as a massage therapist.

"Even at the spa," Brinn confirmed and sat back down at the table. "It's just that no one around here can see them except for me apparently. Don't worry. Most are harmless. The one I saw going into the spa yesterday followed her husband. She was muttering something about making sure her husband didn't end up with a happy ending."

"Seriously?" Hope asked, covering her mouth as she chuckled.

"Yep. I swear the seniors around here are more obsessed with sex than anyone I've ever met," Brinn said, staring at the plate of pastries. While sugar had seemed like a good idea before, now her stomach turned at the thought.

"That might be TMI," Hope said.

"You said it, sister," Yvette agreed. "I wasn't expecting you today. Did you stop by for something specific or because you missed your big sister?"

"I just wanted a free pumpkin scone," she said, reaching over to take one off the tray.

Yvette snorted. "I should've known. Freeloader."

They both laughed. After Hope took a bite, she said, "Actually, I'm headed to Vegas to catch Levi's concert and wanted to pick up a few notebooks for him. For songwriting."

"Vegas? And you didn't invite your favorite sister?" Yvette asked.

"It's a last-minute thing," Hope said. "He's... Well, he seems a little bit off. I think he and Silas had a fight, and I just want to be there to support him."

"Fight?" Brinn asked. "They aren't even in the same country right now, are they?"

"No, they aren't," Hope confirmed with a sigh. "I think that's part of the problem. And those damned gossip rags don't help at all. Silas was supposed to be in Vegas for this show but canceled last minute, right at the same time all the entertainment sites started running stories about him and his costar."

Yvette placed her hands on her hips and scowled. "Those stories better not be true. I'll kick Silas's ass myself."

"Everyone knows you can't trust those gossip sites," Brinn said, praying that was true. Levi and Silas were perfect for each other. If they broke up, she was going to lose faith in romance altogether.

"I don't think they are, but you know how long-distance is. And they both are so busy, Levi with his tour and Silas filming up in Canada. It's no wonder the paparazzi is frothing at the bit for any cracks in their relationship. I'm sure it drives plenty of clicks."

Yvette shook her head. "Why can't they just leave people alone? I have no idea why anyone wants to be famous. I can't imagine having my personal business splashed all over the internet all the time." She walked over to a table that had a stack of notebooks and handed a couple to Hope. "Take these. Tell Levi we want a demo of his new songs."

Hope chuckled. "I'll tell him, but don't count on it. He won't even let me hear anything until he and Seth have recorded the final version."

"Figures. Even family can't get a sneak peek." Yvette smirked and then turned her attention back to Brinn. "What are you going to do?"

"About what?" Brinn asked, wishing the day were over already.

"About Austin? Are you going to call him?"

Both women seemed to move closer to Brinn as they waited for her answer. She'd been trying to put her grandmother's words out of her mind. She didn't want to deal with her issue, though she knew she'd have to sooner rather than later. Brinn started to shake her head, but at that moment, two new ghosts appeared, both of them making a beeline straight for Brinn. She gritted her teeth, knowing the moment of truth had caught up to her, and pulled out her phone.

After hitting the Call button, the phone rang just once before Austin answered. "Brinn. Hey," he said with a smile in his tone. "This is a surprise."

You have no idea, she thought. After clearing her throat, she got right to the point. "I need a favor."

"Anything."

"I need to stay with you for a few days while I figure out how to manage this ghost thing."

He was silent for a moment. Then he sucked in an audible breath. "Of course. Are you coming over now?"

"I need to get Buffy, Willow, and Xander. Will Oz be okay with that? I don't want to leave them alone." Her palms were sweaty and she couldn't believe she was asking to stay with Austin. But if her grandmother was correct, she really had no choice.

"Sure. He likes cats. It's no problem."

"Thank you," she whispered, suddenly overcome with emotion. This was the man she'd fallen in love with all those years ago. The fact that she could call him and ask such a favor, and he'd said yes with no questions asked, was overwhelming. It was a gift she had no idea how to repay.

"You don't have to thank me," he said, his voice going rough. "I'm happy to help. You know that."

She nodded, although she knew he couldn't see her. "I'll be over soon."

"I'll get dinner ready."

When she ended the call, both Yvette and Hope were

staring at her with hearts in their eyes. "Stop it," she ordered. "We're just friends."

"Mmm-hmmm," Yvette said, her eyes dancing with mischief. "Just friends. That's what Hope said about Chad. Now look at them."

Hope rolled her eyes. "At least I didn't marry my boss."

"He wasn't my boss, he was my business partner," Yvette explained while rolling her eyes.

"If you say so." Hope reached over and hugged Brinn. "We're here for you if you need anything. Remember that."

"Thanks," Brinn said, relieved they'd dropped the line of questioning about Austin. Brinn didn't have any answers. She just knew she needed a break. And Austin was her only choice.

CHAPTER 12

*B*rinn stood at Austin's door with three cat carriers at her feet and an overnight bag slung over one shoulder. She still didn't know how she'd gotten to his house. After work, she'd rushed home to pack and corral her cats, but while she was there, two more ghosts showed up and no matter how much she ignored them, they would not go away.

The drive from her house to Austin's was a blur of irritating chatter as one of the ghosts rode along with her. It was a minor miracle she hadn't gotten into an accident.

"I'm telling you, there's money buried in my ex's backyard," the thin woman with electric blue hair cut into an edgy bob insisted. "I was on my way to dig it up when that semi came out of nowhere. I need you to go get it before he finds it. If he gets his hands on that money, he will absolutely do something crazy like spend it all on garden gnomes and name them after everyone from Schitt's Creek."

"So what if he does? Seems harmless to me," Brinn said as she knocked on the door. "It's not like you can do anything with the money now."

"I had plans for that cash!" she yelled, her face contorted into pure rage. "I was going to travel and write a book and donate to charities. You know, interesting things. Not get creepy garden gnomes and then try to spell them to life like some sort of miniature army."

Brinn shuddered. That did sound creepy. But no way was she going to break into some guy's yard and dig around for a cash box that may or may not still be there. "I'm sorry, I can't help you."

"You witch!" the ghost screamed as she picked up a rock from near the front porch and hurled it at Brinn.

The door swung open just as Brinn jumped back and gasped, "What the hell!"

The rock flew by, barely missing her. She turned to the ghost, enraged. "Have you lost your mind?"

"I'm dead!" The ghost screamed. "Of course I've lost my mind!"

"Brinn?" Austin asked as he reached down for the cat carriers. "What's going on?"

"A ghost is screaming at me." She glanced to where the spirit was standing a few feet from her. The ghost's form was starting to fade, but she was still screaming obscenities at Brinn.

"Come in. Let's get you inside," Austin said. He'd already set all three of the cat carriers in the entryway. He slipped his hand into hers and tugged her into the house.

"You can't get away from—"

The moment Brinn stepped into the house, the ghost disappeared. Brinn dropped her overnight bag and without thinking, she slumped against Austin, relieved when his arms wrapped around her. How long had it been since she'd felt safe? She had no idea. And even though her mind was screaming that taking comfort from Austin was a bad idea, she didn't care. This was what she needed. His embrace. His warmth. Him.

"How long has that been going on?" Austin asked.

"How long has what been going on? Ghosts following me around?"

"That and the fact that one seemed to be trying to assault you."

"Uh, they've been haunting me for three, four days?" Brinn reluctantly pulled herself from his embrace. If she stood there too long, all her boundaries would be shattered. "The rock throwing is new. That one must've had a lot of energy in reserve. Most don't have the strength to actually move objects, much less hurl something at me."

Austin glanced around. "Are they gone now?"

Brinn nodded and then felt a small, warm, fuzzy body pressing against her leg. She glanced down and found Oz staring up at her, patiently waiting. Her lips curved into a small smile as she reached down and picked him up. "Hey, buddy."

Oz licked her cheek and snuggled into her chest.

Brinn closed her eyes, enjoying the snuggle from the Lhasa Apso. "You're the sweetest, you know that, right?"

He tilted his head, staring up at her with adoring eyes.

"Look at him, hamming this up," Austin said with a chuckle. "Let's see how he deals with Buffy, Willow, and Xander." Austin made himself busy freeing the cats from their carriers. Willow and Xander took off immediately, but Buffy wound herself between his legs, loving on him in much the same way Oz was with Brinn. "Hey, sweetheart," Austin said, kneeling down to scratch her ears. "I missed you."

The cat purred loudly as she tilted her head, loving the attention.

Brinn watched the pair for a moment, her heart swelling at the love Austin was giving her kitty. Oz started to squirm. "Okay, dude. I'll put you down. You remember Buffy, right?"

Oz's feet hit the floor, and he immediately walked over to Buffy, sniffing her. She stood perfectly still, letting the dog do his thing, and then rubbed against Oz the same way she had against Austin.

Brinn let out a sigh of relief. She hadn't really expected any problems with Oz and the cats interreacting, but they hadn't seen each other in a long time. One never knew how things were going to go. If it had been a problem, Brinn wasn't sure what she would've done.

"Come on," Austin said, slipping his hand around hers. "Let me show you to your room, and then I'll get dinner started."

As Austin led Brinn upstairs, Brinn's hand tingled from his touch. Warmth spread through her until it coiled in her belly, making her press her free hand to her abdomen. Now was not the time for butterflies. She was just there to escape the spirits, so she could function until she could figure out how to control her gift on her own.

But the closer they got to Austin's bedroom, the more she felt that tug of desire she'd always had for him. She couldn't keep her gaze from skimming his body as she remembered all the times they'd spent wrapped around each other in his bed. Her body felt flushed as images of his naked form flashed in her mind, and her fingers itched to glide over his well-defined shoulders, his eight pack abs, and even his forearms. Ms. Betty had been right. There was just something about a man's forearms that was sexy as hell.

Austin came to a stop in front of his room, and she was so lost in her fantasies that she'd nearly walked right into him.

"Whoa," he said gently as he steadied her with both hands.

She quickly took a step back as his touch sent bolts of electricity over her skin. "Sorry. I wasn't expecting…" She glanced at his room. "I mean, I thought we were headed to the guest room."

He blinked. "This is the guest room. Or at least one of them."

Brinn peered in. The bedroom furniture had been replaced since he'd lived there, with a cream-colored wood bedroom set giving it an airy feel. The bedspread was white and accented with green and blue pillows. A couple of Peggy's paintings hung on the walls, making them the focal points of the room. "It's lovely," Brinn said. "But if it's a guest room, where are you sleeping?"

He jerked his head toward the end of the hall. "I took over my grandmother's room after I packed up all her things."

Of course he had. This was his house now. Obviously, he'd take the master bedroom. "Right. That makes sense."

"Do you want a tour?" he asked.

She dropped her overnight bag onto a chair in the corner and shrugged. "Sure." Anything to get out of the room where they'd shared so many moments together.

Austin took her across the hall to the other guest room. It had new furniture too, and was much more masculine than her room. It was filled with dark mahogany furniture, a beige bedspread, and nature photography, most of it in black and white.

"This is where my father stays when he comes back here," Austin said, his tone flat.

"Does he come often?" she asked, surprised. After he'd left town a few years ago, Brinn hadn't heard much about Austin's dad.

"No. He came home about once a year to visit my

grandmother after he left town. He hasn't been back yet since her passing." Austin shut the door and moved quickly down the hall to the opposite end where Xander was sitting in the middle of an open doorway. "Who's this?" Austin asked as he kneeled down to offer his hand to the cat.

"Xander." Brinn squatted down and scratched the cat's head. "Xander, meet Austin. He's our host for a few days. Austin, meet Xander. He's the goofy one of the bunch."

"As he should be," Austin said with a laugh, and Brinn was happy to see his mood was improving. He gave Xander attention for a few moments, and when Xander slinked into the room, Austin waved for Brinn to follow him.

The moment Brinn walked in, she knew this was Austin's private space. His guitar was leaning against the wall next to a writer's desk. There were Post-its stuck to a corkboard on the wall, all with bits of random scribble that she knew were ideas for music he'd yet to write. There was an oversized bean bag chair in the corner that looked well used with a couple of tennis balls on the floor beside it. That's where he did most of his contemplating when he had something on his mind.

Then she turned to the massive king-sized bed. It was made up with a black bedspread and a fuzzy gray blanket at the end. Crisp white pillows were stacked four deep with no colorful throw pillows in sight. She turned and gave him an amused smile. "Some things never change, right?"

He was staring down at her with an intense expression on his face. "You're right. Some things never change." He brought his hand up and brushed a lock of hair back, tucking it behind her ear. "Circumstances, change. But what's in here?" He touched his fingers to her chest, just over her heart. "This rarely does."

Brinn swallowed hard. Tears were burning the backs of her

eyes, but she willed herself to hold it together. "Austin," she whispered. "We can't do this."

"Do what?" he asked, searching her gaze. "Be honest with each other? My feelings for you are as strong as they ever were. You should know that."

This was way too much. Brinn quickly stepped back, breaking their connection. She instantly felt a chill come over her, and she wrapped her arms around herself. "I can't do this. Not now. Not if I'm going to stay here for a few days."

Austin shoved his hands into the pockets of his jeans. "Do what? Listen to my truth? I'm not asking you for anything, Brinn. Not now. I just... I can't have you stay here and not tell you how I feel. You deserve to know."

Ugh. When he put it that way, she felt childish for shutting him down. He was right, he hadn't asked her for anything. But when he said things like that, it made her resolve to keep their relationship platonic all but disappear. She blew out a breath. "Okay. It's just hard for me to process everything right now." And while that wasn't her biggest issue, she was being completely honest. "Can we just take a step back from us and our history for a minute? I need to get my bearings, and having you say things like that... it's a lot."

He nodded. "Yeah. Okay. I get that. I guess just being up here with you brought back more memories than I expected. I'm sorry." Austin quickly turned and headed for the door. "The bathroom in the hall has fresh towels in the closet if you want to freshen up or shower or anything. I'll be downstairs working on dinner."

"Thanks." Brinn followed him out of the room and watched him disappear down the stairs. As soon as she heard his feet hit the hardwood, she sat down on the top step and buried her face in her hands. She didn't blame him for the intimate moment in his bedroom. The truth was, she'd been feeling the same as he had. So much of the past had rushed back in, reminding her of what they'd had together. Her heart ached to be with him again. Everything inside of her did.

But how could she just fall right back into what they'd had before when her life was a gigantic mess? And what about when Austin left town again? That was something she just couldn't face. Though now that ghosts were plaguing her even in Keating Hollow, she'd no longer be tied to the town. If he left, she *could* go with him.

Still, it wasn't just that Austin had left town; it was that he'd left *her*. And deep down, she knew that was the hurt she'd never gotten over. There was no moving forward past friendship until she figured out how to forgive him.

The pitter-pat of dog nails on the wood below caught her attention, and when Oz started to bound up the stairs toward her, his eyes lit with excitement, Brinn smiled at him and held her arms out. He ran, leaping past the last few stairs and jumping right into her arms. She laid back on the landing with Oz on her chest, his tail wagging and his tongue slathering her with kisses.

Brinn let out a giggle and let the dog love on her until he finally hopped off and ran back down the stairs, no doubt ready for a treat. She got up, stopped in the bathroom to wash her face and hands, and then followed her first love back down into the kitchen where he sat waiting patiently near the pantry.

Austin glanced over at her from the kitchen island where he was chopping an onion. "They're on the second shelf."

Oz let out an impatient bark.

Brinn laughed, pulled out a treat for the dog, and then moved to stand next to Austin. "What are we making, and how can I help?"

He handed her another knife and pointed at the pile of vegetables in front of him. "Stir fry."

"With crab fried rice?" she asked hopefully.

He laughed. "Is there any other way?"

Brinn grinned and got to work.

CHAPTER 13

*a*ustin watched Brinn as she sliced a red bell pepper. It was surreal to have her standing in his kitchen cooking with him. There'd been no hesitation on his part when she'd called and asked to stay with him for a few days. How could there be? He'd do anything for her.

He had, however, vowed to himself that he'd keep their relationship in the friend zone. And what had he done? Not ten minutes after she'd walked in the door, he'd told her that he still loved her. *Idiot.*

What was he trying to do? Freak her out? Make her so uncomfortable that she no longer wanted to stay with him? That's exactly what he'd almost done. He hadn't meant to, but standing there with her in his room, he'd been transported back to a time when they'd meant everything to each other. When he'd been able to pour his heart out to her, and she'd done the same.

But things weren't the same. He'd hurt her. Badly. Sure, he'd had his reasons, but that was no excuse for leaving her the way he did. Now if they were going to have a second chance, he needed to earn her trust and let her come to him. It was just so damned hard when all he wanted to do was wrap his arms around her and promise to love her forever.

He'd made that promise before and broken it.

Words were cheap.

It was time to prove to her that he did love her, and he'd do it on her terms. As a friend until and unless she asked him for more.

"I still miss those chicken canisters," Brinn said.

"This kitchen is never going to have chickens again," Austin said, giving her major side-eye.

She laughed. "Where's your sense of adventure?"

"You're kidding, right?" he asked, his lips curving into a smirk. "If it's adventure you want, I'm definitely your man. My bucket list includes balloon rides, skydiving, rock climbing, writing a hit song, scoring movies, and…"

"And what?" she asked, narrowing her eyes at him.

"And… let's save that one for later. How about you? What's on your bucket list?"

Brinn finished with the bell pepper and put her knife down. "Nothing as exciting as all that. I'll do the balloon ride, but the rest? Not really in my wheelhouse."

"You could skydive," Austin said.

"I could, but why would I want to?" She made a face that implied he was crazy.

Austin chuckled as he added the vegetables to his pan and doused them in soy sauce. "For the adrenaline rush?"

"I get my adrenaline rushes from dodging ghosts these days. I don't need any more excitement."

"Fair." Austin got busy finishing up their dinner while Brinn set the table and poured them both a glass of wine.

Once they were seated across from each other, Brinn raised

her glass. "To finally getting dinner. It's not crab cakes, but it'll do."

Austin smiled at her and touched his glass to hers. "To finally getting dinner. We'll do crab cakes tomorrow."

Brinn beamed. "I can't wait."

After they finished dinner and did the dishes, Austin was drying his hands when he glanced over at Brinn and found her hovering awkwardly on the other side of the Island. Their eyes met, and she glanced away quickly.

"I guess I'll go check on the cats," Brinn said. "Make sure they are all okay, and then head up to my room."

Austin glanced at the clock. It wasn't even eight yet. "It's still early. I was going to find a movie to watch. Oz likes to curl up next to me on the couch before we call it a night. "You're welcome to join us."

"Oh, uh, yeah," she stammered and then squeezed her eyes shut as she shook her head. A nervous laugh escaped her lips before she said, "I don't know why I'm so... never mind. I'm going to check on the cats. Then I'll either crack open a book or come down and see what you and Oz are watching."

"Okay. I hope you do." Austin watched her leave the kitchen. Once he heard her footsteps on the stairs, he pressed his hands down on the counter and hung his head. He'd had no idea how hard it would be to have her in his space and not be with her. All he wanted to do was follow her up those stairs, but instead, he blew out a breath, made himself a cup of coffee, and went to find Oz.

His dog was curled up in his dog bed at the end of the couch, but as soon as he heard Austin coming, his head popped up.

"Hey, boy," Austin said as he sat at the end of the couch. "Ready to watch a movie?"

Oz ran over around the coffee table, took a flying leap, and landed with all four paws sprawled out on the cushion next to Austin.

Austin let out a bark of laughter. "You silly pup. Come here." He patted the couch and Oz immediately curled up next to him. With one hand petting his dog and the remote in the other, he turned the TV on.

After scrolling mindlessly, he finally clicked on a rom-com he knew Brinn liked. He got as far as two women deciding to house swap before his eyes started to close.

"Hey," Brinn said into Austin's ear.

His eyes flew open and he glanced around, spotting Brinn sitting next to him with Oz now curled up in her lap. "Hey yourself."

She reached over to grab the remote.

"I thought you liked *The Holiday*," he said.

Brinn laughed. "I do. But the movie's over. I figured I'd pick something you might like this time."

Austin blinked at the television. The credits were rolling. He snorted and turned to her. "How long have you been sitting here?"

"About an hour."

Damn. He'd missed a whole hour of sharing the couch with her as they watched one of her favorite movies. "You could've woken me up sooner."

"Why? You looked so peaceful napping with Oz." She smiled down at his dog. "I did drink your coffee though, so I hope you're up for another movie, cause I'm not going to sleep anytime soon."

He glanced at his empty mug on the coffee table and felt his heart swell slightly. How many times in the past had she stolen his coffee when he wasn't paying attention? "Looks like I need a refill," he said as he got up and grabbed his mug. "Can I get you anything?"

Brinn shrugged one shoulder. "I guess I'm fine."

"There's ice cream. Chocolate peanut butter crunch."

"You're not messing with me, are you?" Brinn asked with her eyes narrowed.

"Do you really think I'd do that?"

She raised one eyebrow. "It wouldn't be the first time."

He chuckled. "You might be right about that, but this time it is true. Are you in?"

"Absolutely." She glanced down at Oz. "I'd come help you, but…"

He laughed. "Don't get up. I've got it."

Five minutes later, Austin returned with a tray of ice cream and coffee.

"You might just be my hero," Brinn said as she took one of the bowls of ice cream.

Austin took his spot on the couch and watched as Oz sprawled out between them and laid his head on Brinn's thigh. Traitor. Oz had always preferred Brinn over him, given the choice. Shaking his head, he grabbed his ice cream and felt whole for the first time in years.

Brinn took a big bite of the ice cream and moaned her pleasure. "This is delicious."

So are you, he wanted to say, but kept it to himself. Instead, he just nodded and ignored his own bowl as he continued to watch her.

She took another spoonful and eyed him. "You're not eating."

Oh, he was. He was eating up everything she had to offer in that moment. "I'll get to it."

"It's going to melt."

"Hmm." He grabbed the spoon and ate a few bites but was too interested in watching her to finish his own.

"If you're not going to eat that, I'll take it," she said when her bowl was empty.

He didn't hesitate to hand his bowl over. Then he grabbed his coffee and sipped as he enjoyed the Brinn show.

"I put *Tombstone* on for you," she said.

He glanced at the television and spotted Doc Holliday at the poker table. His lips curved into a pleased smile. He'd chosen one of her favorite rom-coms, and she'd chosen one of his favorite westerns. "Thanks."

"Anytime."

He finished his coffee and sat with his arm draped across the back of the couch. It wasn't long before Oz jumped down to the floor and curled up into his dog bed as he did most nights when he was tired of cuddling.

"Guh, he's so damned cute," Brinn said when Oz curled up into a ball, just the way he had when he was a puppy.

"He is," Austin agreed. "Are the cats settled in okay?"

"Yep. I set up their litter box in the guest room and put some water out for them. When I left, Buffy and Willow were curled up on my bed and Xander was prowling the hallway. Don't be surprised if you find he's commandeered your pillow. It's one of his favorite things to do."

"I can share, just as long as he doesn't mind me and Oz," Austin said.

"I'm sure it won't be an issue. That cat doesn't care about much as long as he has a good pillow and someone to feed him treats."

"Sounds like a man after my own heart," Austin said.

"He does, doesn't he?" She winked at him and then yawned.

"There's coffee," he said, nodding to the mug she hadn't touched.

"No. I'll never get to sleep if I have another. You can have it."

Never one to pass up coffee, Austin reached over and grabbed the mug.

Silence fell between them as they each watched the movie. But Austin was hyper aware of the woman sitting next to him. And when she slumped down into the couch toward him, he laid a pillow in his lap and patted it, inviting her to lie down.

She glanced up at him with sleepy eyes, smiled softly, and then curled up with her head in his lap.

Austin felt the last of the tension leave his body. He'd happily stay in every night if he had Brinn with him just like this. He rested his hand on her head and ran his fingers gently through her hair.

Brinn sighed in contentment. "I like that."

"I know."

CHAPTER 14

*B*rinn followed Oz down the stairs the next morning. He scampered into the kitchen where they found Austin standing at the stove cooking pancakes.

"Well, good morning," Brinn said as she made a beeline for the coffee pot. "Are we having guests for breakfast?"

He chuckled. "No. Just us."

She eyed the giant stack of pancakes he'd already cooked. "I hope three-quarters of those are for you."

"Nope. Just half. Hope you brought your stretchy pants, cause chef Austin is going to fatten you up."

"You wish."

He was still chuckling as he turned the stove off and handed her a plate.

With her mouth-watering, Brinn took a couple of pancakes and sat at the table. When Austin joined her, she stared at him for a moment.

"What?"

She took a bite before answering. "I'm just wondering if

this is what you're always like or if you're just trying to impress me."

"What do you mean 'always like?'"

"This." She waved her fork at the pancakes. "You made me dinner, brought me dessert, and now you've made me breakfast. Do you always cook, or is this just because I'm here?"

"What if I said I always cook? That this is just a normal day?" he asked.

"Then I'm moving in permanently," she quipped. But the moment the words were spoken, she covered her mouth with her free hand.

Austin grinned at her. "I'll get you a full set of keys today."

"Stop. You know that was just hyperbole." She stuffed another bite of pancakes into her mouth.

"It doesn't have to be," he said, and although he'd kept his tone light and teasing, she could sense the seriousness beneath the surface.

Brinn put her fork down. "Tell me what's next for you."

"Next?" He followed her lead and stopped eating. Instead, he picked up his coffee mug and held it in two hands as he watched her.

"Yes. Next. After your done closing your grandmother's estate? What are you doing with the house?" *When are you leaving to go back to your recording studio?* That's what she really wanted to know but couldn't bring herself to ask.

"I'm keeping the house. I thought you knew that." His brows pinched together as he frowned at her.

She shrugged. "I figured you would, but since you work down south, you might not want to deal with maintaining it."

"No one said I was going to live down south forever," he said. "Besides, Gideon and I have decided to use my grandmother's money to form a kid's nonprofit arts program."

Brinn stared at him, her eyes wide. "Wow. That's… just wow. It's very generous of you both."

"My grandmother would've loved it."

"Yes, she would have," Brinn agreed. "Is it going to be a summer thing, or…?"

"Year round, right here in Keating Hollow." His features softened as he continued. "We need to get together and work out more details, but the general idea is that Gideon is going to oversee the art program, and I'm going to oversee the music program."

Brinn suddenly teared up and blinked rapidly to hold them back. Her heart was full. She'd always known Austin was a good man with a kind heart. But she hadn't realized his heart was made of gold. She reached across the table and covered his hand with hers and squeezed. "I think it's amazing. The world needs more people like you."

Austin's cheeks flushed pink, making Brinn's heart melt even further. Dammit. She was doomed. Her so-called boundaries were nothing more than a thin piece of cardboard that were on the edge of collapse. Why was she denying herself this man again?

Right. The fact that he'd crushed her before and had the power to do it again and again and again. If she let her guard down, it meant risking that crushing blow again, and she just didn't know if she could do it.

"I don't know if that's true about the world needing more of me. I just want to make sure kids have the opportunity to explore their creative sides."

Brinn knew how important that was to him, especially considering how his father had always discouraged his interest in music. "It's true," she said definitively. "I'm sure your program is going to be hugely popular. Let me know if there's anything I can do."

He nodded. "I will."

She wanted to ask if that meant he'd be in Keating Hollow more often but stopped herself. What would she say if he said yes?

"What about you?" he asked. "What are your plans?"

"Plans for what?" She picked her fork back up and started cutting into her pancakes. "Work? I'll be at the bookstore for as long as Yvette wants me. I love it there."

"I can see that," he said with a small nod. "But I was really inquiring about your ghost problem. It seems that your grandmother was right. They don't bother you here?"

"They haven't since I walked in yesterday." She picked up her coffee and sat back in the chair. "That's a huge relief. I can't tell you how exhausting it is to listen to them all the time. I just hope I can find someone to help me control this *gift*, as my grandmother calls it, soon. I can't stay here forever."

Austin opened his mouth to say something but then quickly closed it.

"What?" she asked.

"Nothing."

Brinn narrowed her eyes. "It's not nothing. What were you going to say?"

He glanced away, his gaze focusing on Oz, who was curled up with Willow in a dog bed in the corner. Finally he turned back to her. "You're welcome to stay here as long as you want to. That's all."

Butterflies fluttered in her stomach, making her press her hand to her belly. *Stop it*, she ordered herself. It was on the tip of her tongue to tell him she couldn't do that. That she'd leave tomorrow even if she still had no idea how to block out her ghosts. But she didn't. She couldn't. Instead, she nodded and said, "Thank you. I appreciate that. I'm waiting to hear from Abby and Bree to see if I can find someone or something to help me. Hopefully, they'll come through with somewhere to start other than relying on your hospitality."

He leaned forward. "I imagine Bree is working on a spell or potion of some sort. What is Abby is doing? Something similar?"

"No, she's trying to contact some friends in New Orleans who might know what else I can do besides cloak myself in sage to ward off the ghosts. She said she knew a couple of mediums down there."

"That sounds like a start," Austin said. "Seems like there are probably a lot of ghosts down there."

Brinn snorted. "Yeah. Apparently they are everywhere. It's a shame, since visiting New Orleans was on my bucket list, but it seems that's not going to happen."

"That is a shame. Imagine the fun we'd have there." He winked and got up to grab a pad of paper and a pen that was sitting on the counter. When he returned to his seat, he scribbled something at the top and asked, "What else is on your bucket list?"

"Why?" She peered at the paper. He'd written *Brinn's Bucket List* at the top.

"We talked about the things that were on mine, now I want to know what things are on yours. Maybe we can tackle a few while you're staying with me."

That was just one of the many reasons she'd fallen in love with this man. "Okay, my bucket list, in no particular order, starts with making everything in *The Witch's Guide to Chocolate and Pastries*."

"A chocolate and pastry challenge," he said as he wrote it down. "I'm in. We'll make at least one thing a day. Is today too soon to start?"

She laughed. "Nope. I also want to learn to play the guitar, plant a sunflower garden, write a book, learn to weld, and build a treehouse."

He scribbled them all down and then looked up at her. "No travel or professional dreams?"

Brinn's smile vanished, and suddenly she didn't want to play this game anymore. She got up and took her half-eaten pancakes to the garbage. After scraping her plate, she loaded it into the dishwasher and then just stood at the sink, hating her reaction. He'd merely asked a question, and she'd turned into a sullen teenager instead of just answering.

"Brinn?" he asked from right behind her.

How had she not even heard him get up and cross the kitchen? "Yeah?"

He wrapped his hand around her wrist and gently turned her to face him. "I'm sorry."

"What do you have to be sorry for? You've been nothing but kind to me."

"For making you uncomfortable." His whiskey-colored eyes were full of sincerity. "That wasn't my intention. I just want to know you again. That's all."

"I know." She stared up at him, holding his gaze. "I never let myself think about travel or even what else I might do. I never intended to leave Keating Hollow, and short of starting my own business, which I have zero capital to do, there just aren't that many opportunities. So I don't think about it."

He nodded. "I get it. How about we just focus on your list as is? I have a great tree that would be perfect for a treehouse. Want to go take a look?"

She gaped at him. "You can't be serious."

"Sure I am." He shrugged one shoulder. "The house sits on a few acres of land. Might as well do something fun with it."

Brinn shook her head and laughed. "Okay. Let's go see this tree."

He grabbed her hand and led her toward the back door. As soon as Oz heard the door open, he jumped up out of the bed and nearly tripped Brinn as he darted out the door.

"Jeez, Oz. Why don't you just knock me over next time," Brinn said, rolling her eyes at the dog's exuberance.

"Don't tempt him." Austin followed her out into the sun-drenched backyard. "He's tried it with me more than once."

"I bet." Brinn glanced around at the neatly maintained property. There were raised flower gardens with a cobblestone walkway winding through them. "This is gorgeous. Do you maintain it, or do you have a gardener?" She was willing to bet her entire paycheck he'd hired a gardener. How could he possibly have enough time to keep it looking so perfectly manicured?

"I do it. Or at least I have since I've been back in town."

Brinn just stared at him. "Seriously?"

He nodded. "It helps me relax." Then he pointed to a particularly sunny space that looked to have been recently cleared. "When the weather is right, we can plant your sunflowers there. Roses used to be in that spot, but the deer ate them."

"Oh." She cleared her throat. "I was going to plant them at my house."

"That makes sense. I'll put some there anyway. Sunflowers always remind me of you."

Her face heated, and it wasn't from the weak January sun. "They'll look lovely there."

"Agreed. This way." He took her hand and together, with Oz trotting along with them, they made their way through the garden into a patch of redwood trees. "There." He pointed to a large tree that stood off by itself in the northwest corner of his property. "There's plenty of room for a decent treehouse, don't you think?"

Brinn walked over to the tree, pressed her hands to the rough bark, and let the calming energy soothe her. She'd always felt most at peace among the trees. Or she had until a ghost suddenly appeared about ten feet away. Brinn bristled, waiting for the man to approach or speak to her. He'd passed young. Maybe early thirties. But he was dressed in slacks, a white button-down shirt, and suspenders, complete with a fedora hat, making her think he was from the nineteen-fifties era.

But instead of engaging her, the ghost stood where he was, took his hat off and pressed it to his chest, while mouthing what appeared to be a prayer. When he was done, he placed a single daisy at the base of one of the trees and then walked back into the forest.

Brinn turned to Austin. "Did you see that?"

He nodded, his gaze still focused in the direction of where the ghost had been. "Did you hear what he said?"

She shook her head. "No. Did you?"

"No." He turned to look her in the eye. "But it looked like he said, 'For my love, Margaret.'"

"Who's Margaret?"

"My grandmother. Peggy is short for Margaret." He walked the ten feet over to the tree, and Brinn followed him.

She stared down at the daisy, it's petals bright white against the red forest floor.

"Look." Austin reached out and touched the trunk of the

tree. Just above his fingers were a pair of initials carved in the tree inside a heart. *BD + MC.*

"Do you know what the initials stand for?" Brinn asked.

"I have no idea who BD is, but MC could be my grandmother. Her maiden name was Carlisle."

"Whoa," Brinn squeezed his hand. "That man we saw definitely wasn't your grandfather. He was far too tall." And far too good looking if Brinn was being honest. Stewart Steele had passed when Brinn was about twelve years old. He'd always been active in the Keating Hollow community, and everyone had known him. He had a reputation for being a bit ruthless in business, but generous to his neighbors.

"No, he definitely wasn't my grandfather." Austin was silent as he walked back to the tree he'd picked out for the treehouse. When she joined him, he said, "So? Are you up for building a treehouse?"

"Uh, sure? I don't have the slightest clue where to start, but I'm game if you are."

"YouTube," he said and wrapped his arm around her shoulders. "And when we're done, we'll both sign our initials to the tree." He flashed her a playful smile. "The heart is optional."

Brinn rolled her eyes, but deep down, she knew that was the moment when her cardboard boundaries had collapsed.

There was no denying that she was head over heels in love with him... again. Or maybe still. But when he left again, no matter what walls she tried to create, her heart would be shattered. If that was the case, she might as well jump in with both feet. "Hey, Austin?"

"Yeah?"

She stepped right in front of him, forcing them both to stop.

He stared down at her, his expression morphing from

concerned to understanding as she pressed her palms to his chest and licked her lips. His gaze moved to her mouth, and his voice was gruff when he asked, "Is this when we get to stop pretending that we're just friends?"

Brinn nodded, pressed up onto her tiptoes, and brushed her lips over his. Tingles rushed over her skin at the feathery contact. But when his arms wrapped around her, tugging her close, she opened to him, tasting him. One of her hands found the back of his neck while the other cupped his cheek. And then both hands were in his hair as the kiss turned heated, their passion igniting a flame they'd kept simmering for more than five years.

CHAPTER 15

*A*ustin pulled Brinn against him, reveling in the feel of her body molded to his. Everything else faded away, and the only thing that mattered to him was having the love of his life back in his arms.

Brinn stilled, and with her lips against his, she asked, "Did you hear that?"

"No more ghosts. Not right now," he insisted.

"No, not ghosts. I thought I heard Oz."

Austin jerked away from Brinn and glanced around. His dog had been right beside them just moments ago. But now, he was nowhere in sight. "Oz!" he called.

A very faint barking sounded in the distance.

"This way." Austin took off through the trees to the other side of the property. He periodically called out for the Lhasa, but there was no sign of him and the barking had ceased. That, more than anything, was what sent Austin into a mild panic. If his dog was chasing something or threatened, he'd be barking his fool head off.

"Any sight of him?" Brinn puffed out from right behind him.

"No." Austin scanned the forest floor, searching for a patch of white. Nothing. His dog was nowhere to be seen.

"Oz!" Brinn called and split off from Austin's path.

He heard the panic in her voice and had to block out horrible images of predators who might have found him. The area was known for eagles, bobcats, and even the occasional bear. Austin never took his dog out without keeping a close eye on him, but this time, *this one time*, he'd forgotten all about Oz when he'd had Brinn in his arms.

His stomach rolled, and he had to force the images out of his mind.

"There!" Brinn yelled and pointed toward a sunny patch in a clearing.

"Oz, what are you…" Austin slowed and peered at his dog who appeared to be curled up next to another small brindle-colored puppy.

Brinn kneeled down next to the two animals and placed a soft hand on Oz. He lifted his head and looked at her, then lowered it so he was resting his head on the smaller puppy. "Austin, I think this puppy is hurt."

Austin finally reached them and crouched down to first inspect Oz. Relief rushed through him as he determined that Oz was perfectly fine. He appeared to be protecting the puppy. "What's happened here?" he asked Oz. It was no surprise when his dog didn't move. He met Brinn's gaze.

She pointed toward the puppy's back left leg. "It looks like something might have attacked her."

"Damn." Austin inspected the gash on the puppy's leg. She clearly needed to get to the emergency vet or a healer as soon as possible. "Good boy, Oz," he said, petting Oz's head.

"But I need you to get up now. We've got to help your new friend."

Oz got to his feet but hovered near the puppy, nervously fidgeting around the smaller dog.

Austin pulled his sweatshirt off and wrapped the puppy in it.

"Come on, Oz," Brinn said, snapping her fingers. "Let's get home before whatever did that comes back."

Oz trotted along with them as they quickly made their way back to the house. As soon as they had Oz safely indoors, they rushed to Austin's car. He handed her the puppy and jumped into the driver's seat. "Is there a vet in town?"

"Yes. It's just off Main Street."

AUSTIN SPED through town while the puppy whined in Brinn's arms.

"You're okay," Brinn whispered to the puppy, wanting desperately to soothe the shaking dog. No doubt she was in shock. "We've got you now."

The puppy whimpered, and Brinn's heart nearly broke. Why couldn't her gift be one of healing? That would be a lot more useful than seeing ghosts who wanted to rate their past lovers. She cuddled the puppy closer and gently petted her head, making sure she knew she wasn't alone.

Fifteen minutes later, Austin wrapped his arm around Brinn as they waited for an update from the vet.

"Where do you think she came from?" Brinn asked, leaning her head against his shoulder, grateful to have him with her.

"No idea. Usually when puppies are out in the woods like that, it's because someone left them there."

"Who in Keating Hollow would dump a puppy?" she asked, horrified.

He shook his head. "That kind of thing just doesn't happen around here."

But Brinn was barely paying attention to his answer. An older woman had just appeared. She was still wearing her housecoat and was frantically yelling for someone to let her see Ms. Puppy. When no one at the desk acknowledged her, the ghost turned and spotted Brinn staring in her direction. Brinn stiffened, bracing for the onslaught of requests to start.

"What's wrong?" Austin asked.

"A ghost," a woman said from the other side of the waiting room.

Brinn turned and spotted Zya, the owner of Witches in Stitches. When had she come in? "You can see her, too?" Brinn asked.

"Yes." Zya smoothed her long black dress and picked up a pet carrier that was sitting on the floor beside her. She wore lace-up boots that clattered on the tile floor as she made her way toward the door. The elegant woman glanced back at the ghost and then to Brinn as she added, "Good luck with that one."

"Wait!" Brinn called as the other woman disappeared out of the office. Dammit! She desperately wanted to follow Zya out of the office and ask her to explain everything she knew about ghosts, if she saw them all the time, how she handled it, how Brinn was supposed to handle this. But as soon as she started to stand up, the ghost appeared in front of her. Brinn peered around the spirit and spotted Zya in the driver's seat of a black Jeep Wrangler as she sped out of the parking lot. Brinn made a mental note to find Zya as soon as possible.

"You can see me. I know you can," the ghost said, waving

her arms frantically. "You need to find out what happened to Ms. Puppy. Tell them an eagle attacked her. I tried my best to stop it. I hit that damned bird with my shoe."

The ghost lifted her foot, showing off her red and green striped sock. "I guess I startled it, because he let go of my baby and came for me. That's when the pressure on my chest started. I don't know what happened after that. I think I passed out."

"How did you end up here?" Brinn asked.

"I have no idea. All I know is that when I asked the Goddess about Ms. Puppy, she sent me here."

Brinn blinked at the ghost. "The Goddess?"

"Have you seen Ms. Puppy?" the woman asked, her eyes frantic as she glanced around the vet's office.

"Yes. We found her and brought her here," Brinn said. "I'm sorry, but I didn't catch your name."

"Miller. Mrs. Pete Miller. My Pete passed ten years ago. It was just me and Candy Girl for all this time. Well, it was, anyway. Candy Girl crossed the rainbow bridge a couple months ago. I just got Ms. Puppy."

"Right. Mrs. Miller, Ms. Puppy is being seen by the vet. We found her in the woods with a pretty bad wound on one of her hind legs," Brinn said.

"Oh, my poor baby!" she wailed.

Brinn winced.

"What's happening?' Austin asked her as he wrapped his hand around hers.

"Do you have a neighbor named Mrs. Miller?"

"Yes, I think she lives about three houses down. Why?" He grimaced. "Oh no. Is that who you're talking to?"

"Yes." Brinn let out a sigh and slumped against him. She

clutched at his chest, and with a sad tone, she said, "We need to call Drew."

"Damn," he said softly as he pulled out his phone.

He made the call, and when Austin explained how he knew about Mrs. Miller's death, Brinn was grateful they lived in Keating Hollow and his explanation of a ghost was taken in stride.

"They're headed over to her house now," he told Brinn when he got off the phone.

"What did you just say!" the ghost demanded, standing right in front of them.

Brinn steeled herself and stared her right in the eye as she said, "Mrs. Miller, are you aware that you've left your body?"

"What do you mean, left my body? I'm right here." She glanced down at herself and patted her stomach. Except because she was in ghost form, her hand went right through her body. She stood completely still for a few seconds, then moved her hand back and forth and wiggled her fingers, trying to make a connection with her body. Instead, her hand slid through her ghostly form as easily as if she were trying to touch a cloud. She looked up, meeting Brinn's gaze. "I died?"

Brinn nodded sadly. "I'm sorry. I don't know what happened, but it sort of sounds like a heart attack."

"Son of a monkey on a rotating pogo stick! I had a date tonight. I even planned to shave my legs." She fanned herself dramatically. "I was really looking forward to an up close and personal look at Edward's forearms. He used to be a custom cabinet maker. I just keep imagining him with his sleeves rolled up and—"

Mrs. Miller kept moving her lips, but no sound came out as more of her form silently faded from the office.

When the ghost was gone, Brinn sighed and slipped her hand into Austin's. "Looks like Ms. Puppy needs a new home."

"She's got one. Unless Mrs. Miller's family wants her, we'll take her home with us," Austin said.

Home with us. Brinn was almost afraid to admit to herself how good that sounded. She cleared her throat. "She'd be a great sister for Oz."

Austin nodded. "I've been meaning to get him a brother or sister. Looks like one found him."

They sat together with Brinn leaning against his shoulder while they waited for the vet to appear. When she finally walked into the lobby with the puppy in her arms, the puppy's leg was completely wrapped in a bandage and she'd been fitted with a soft Elizabethan collar.

"Hey there, Mom and Dad," the vet said as she handed the puppy to Brinn.

Brinn and Austin shared a look. *Mom and Dad?*

"Baby Steele has had a bit of a rough day, but we've cleaned her wound, stitched her up, and prescribed some antibiotics. She'll need to keep her collar on, and no running, playing, or jumping on that leg for ten days until it's time to get the stitches out. Any questions?"

"Baby Steele?" Austin asked.

The vet's lips tugged up into a smile. "I understand she doesn't have a name yet, so that's what we're going with until you tell us otherwise."

Austin glanced at Brinn. "Cordelia?"

"Drusilla," Brinn said.

"She's gonna need a leather collar."

Brinn cuddled Drusilla closer to her chest and laughed. "I think that can be arranged."

CHAPTER 16

"They're going to be the best of friends," Brinn said, smiling down at Drusilla and Oz. When they'd gotten back to Austin's house, Brinn had placed Drusilla in Oz's dog bed at the end of the couch. It hadn't taken long for Oz to find her there and to curl up around her as he kept a keen eye on his new friend.

"I just talked to Drew." Austin placed his phone on the coffee table. "Mrs. Miller's next of kin is a nephew she hasn't seen since he was five years old."

"How old is he now?" Brinn asked.

"Twenty-one, and he's at college. Drew asked him about the dog, but he's not in a position to care for her."

Brinn knew she shouldn't be happy about the fact that Mrs. Miller didn't have close relatives who wanted Drusilla, but she just couldn't stop herself from smiling down at the sweet girl. She was already in love. "Well, it's a good thing that Baby Steele already has a Mom and Dad ready with open arms.

Austin chuckled. "It is." Then he eyed her for a moment

before he said, "You saw two ghosts today while I was with you."

She nodded. "It appears this house is my only sanctuary."

"I'm not going to complain about that," he said with a self-satisfied smile.

"Unfortunately, I'm going to need to leave this sanctuary because Abby called and wants me to meet her at the brewery, and then I'm going to try to find Zya and see what she knows about ghosts. Like I said before, I can't stay here forever."

"Yes you can." Austin replied so softly she wasn't sure she'd heard him correctly.

"What did you just say?" She stood stock-still, her entire body tingling with nerves.

He cleared his throat and stared her in the eye. "I said you can stay here forever. There's no reason why you can't."

"Come on, Austin. I can't just stay in your house indefinitely. You'll get sick of me sooner or later." She was trying to maintain a carefree tone. Something, *anything* to see her way out of this suddenly very serious conversation.

"No, I won't," he insisted as he moved closer.

"What about when you go back to LA? You're not going to want me here in your space."

"Are you sure about that?" He cupped her cheek with his right hand and brushed back a lock of her hair with his left.

"No," she breathed as she got lost in his intense gaze. "But—"

"But nothing, Brinn." He leaned forward, resting his forehead against hers. "I love having you here, and while I don't have any immediate plans to head back to LA, even if I did, I have no problem with you staying here. Don't you know I'd do anything or give you anything to keep you safe?"

Dammit. Tears were stinging the backs of her eyes again. He was every bit the man she'd fallen in love with years ago, only now he was even better. If he hurt her… She couldn't even think about the possibility. "That's very generous of you."

He let out a small chuckle. "Generous isn't the word I'd use. But sure, let's go with that."

"What would you call it, then?" she asked, pulling back and narrowing her eyes at him.

"Something closer to self-serving." He dropped one hand to her waist and pulled her in close so that their bodies were molded together. "I like having you in my space."

Every part of her felt like it was on fire. This man whom she'd loved for so long was telling her everything she'd longed to hear. And she'd bet everything she had that he meant every word. "Austin?"

"Brinn?"

"I have to go." It nearly killed her to say the words. All she wanted to do was wrap herself around the man she loved and never let go, but she took a step back. "Abby's waiting."

Austin's grip tightened on her waist, and he pulled her into him again.

"I really do need to get going," she said, but melted into him anyway.

His lips curved into a half smile. "You'll get there… eventually." Then he lowered his mouth to hers and kissed her so thoroughly her fingers and toes started to tingle. The world fell away, and the only thing that existed was his touch and the feel of his body against hers.

Just when she was ready to take things a step further, Austin pulled back.

"Where are you going?" she asked, staring at his lips.

"I'm not going anywhere," he said, amused. "But you are. Remember Abby?"

"Oh, damn." She squeezed her eyes shut just so that Austin wasn't in her sightline and finally stepped back, putting some much-needed distance between them.

Austin laughed.

Her eyes flew open, and she glared at him. "What?"

"You're adorable when you're turned on."

"I'm not turned on," she lied.

He just raised one questioning eyebrow.

"Okay, fine. I am. Or was. But now I'm thinking about Abby and ghosts and wondering what crazy spirit is going to bother me when I'm out, so I guess I'm over it."

"Don't worry. I'll be here for a repeat performance when you get back." He walked her to the door.

Brinn glanced back at Drusilla and Oz who were still curled up in the dog bed. "Maybe I should meet with Abby tomorrow. I'm not sure I should be leaving Drusilla after the day she's had."

"I'll be here," Austin reassured her. "Abby's already waiting, right?"

"Yeah, but—"

Austin opened the door, kissed her on the cheek, and said, "Go on."

Brinn sighed. "Okay. But be ready to start making something chocolatey and delicious when I get back. We have that bucket list to work on."

"On it." He kissed her one last time, and by the time he backed away, she had a goofy smile on her face and practically floated to her car.

Austin's house was only a few miles outside of town, but it quickly became apparent that the ride was going to feel like forever. As soon as she left the driveway, Mrs. Miller appeared in the passenger seat.

"You stole my dog," the woman accused.

Brinn glanced over at the ghost, noting her uncombed frizzy hair and yesterday's mascara under her eyes. "We didn't steal her. We've adopted her," Brinn said calmly.

"It's your fault I died!" she cried, clutching at her chest.

"How so?" After the week she'd had, Brinn was so used to ghosts invading her space with their crazy antics that she just wasn't fazed by the accusation.

"Ms. Puppy heard that dog of yours and ran outside. When that eagle attacked her, that's when my heart gave out. This is your fault and you owe me."

"Of course," Brinn muttered. It was on the tip of her tongue to protest the assertion that Oz was her dog, but for some reason she couldn't say the words. They just felt... wrong.

"Ha! Good. Then you agree." She pointed a finger at Brinn. "Since it's your fault I died, I need you to do something for me."

"I don't agree. That was sarcasm."

"A life for a life. That's how I was raised," Mrs. Miller said with an air of superiority.

A life for a life? What was this, *The Sopranos?* "So what are you asking? That I lay down my life for you?"

"No. But I want you to marry my nephew. He needs a good woman in his life."

Brinn snorted. "I thought it was my fault you died. Is that what you call a good woman?"

"Semantics." She waved a hand and made a face. "Good woman or not, he needs to experience life with a woman, not that... *man.* I don't know what his mama was thinking, but she should've never moved him to the Bay Area. If they'd just stayed here, he wouldn't have been corrupted."

"Corrupted?" Brinn parroted as she pulled into a parking space in front of the brewery and then gaped at the ghost. "You want me to date your nephew so that he won't date a man?"

"Yes. That's it." She slumped back into the seat, relief washing over her wrinkled face. "That's exactly it."

"You're a bigot," Brinn said. "Get out of my car."

Mrs. Miller sat up straight, her back rigid, clearly gearing up to give Brinn a piece of her mind.

Brinn held up a hand and with a conviction she didn't know she possessed, she said, "You are not welcome here. Leave now and never bother me or Austin again."

The ghost blinked and then looked down at her hands. Her mouth dropped open, and her eyes were frantic as they both watched her hands crack into a million pieces. The cracking spread quickly, and within seconds, she was gone.

"Holy crow," Brinn whispered, resting her head against her seat.

"Brinn?"

She glanced over and found Abby standing at the driver's side of her car, her eyebrows raised and a concerned expression on her face.

Brinn pushed the door open and climbed out. "Hey, Abby. Sorry I'm late."

"Did you just… I mean, was that a ghost in your car?" Her eyes were wide and full of awe.

"Yeah. It was." Brinn glanced at the brewery. "Can we go in? I need a drink."

Abby chuckled. "I bet you do. Wow. I've never spoken to a ghost before or even interacted with one. That was… impressive."

"More like crazy," Brinn said and followed Abby into the brewery.

Abby led her to a table in the back that offered privacy from the rest of the dining room. "Take a seat. I'll go get us some drinks. Do you have a preference?"

Brinn shook her head. "Whatever you have handy."

"I'm on it."

Brinn folded her arms on the table and then lowered her head, trying to ward off the tension headache forming at the base of her skull. It was virtually unheard of to have a run-in with a homophobe in Keating Hollow. The community had always been accepting of everyone, and to have Mrs. Miller speak about her nephew as if something was wrong with him hit Brinn hard. It made her want to find him and make sure he was okay, that he had a support system. If he came to Keating Hollow to settle her estate, Brinn would be sure to befriend him.

"I got you the new winter porter Clay has been working on. I'm still breastfeeding, so it's just regular old non-alcoholic cider for me. And I put in an order for some buffalo wings and cheese fries," Abby said as she placed two glasses on the table.

"You're a goddess." Brinn grabbed a glass and took a long sip. "Tell Clay this is delicious. In fact, remind me to grab a growler before I go."

Abby grinned. "It's really good, isn't it? I suggested a few spices I love, and I'm pretty sure they made the difference."

"So we should call this Abby's Winter Brew?" Brinn asked, grinning at her friend.

"I like it. I'll be sure to tell Clay to get the labels ready." Abby's expression turned serious when she said, "Okay. Tell me what happened today. How did a ghost end up in your car?"

Brinn took another long sip of her beer and then told Abby the story. When she got to the part about Mrs. Miller being a homophobe, Abby recoiled.

"Oh, no. Not only are you dealing with ghosts bothering you all the time, now you've got one that's a total A-hole, too."

"Pretty much," Brinn said. "But I'm not sure she'll be back. Did you see the way she disengaged? That's new. I've never had that happen before."

"I did see that. Looked pretty permanent to me, but what do I know?" She dug around in her purse and pulled out a card. "The number on the back is a friend of a friend from New Orleans. Bianca Blue. She's a professional medium with her own shop in the Quarter. She might have some insight."

Brinn took the card, glanced at the name and number, and then tucked it into her pocket. "Thank you, Abby. I really appreciate this."

"It's no problem. I can't imagine having to deal with random ghosts following me around all the time. Yvette told me what happened at the bookstore. It sounds so invasive."

"It is," Brinn confirmed. "And exhausting."

Abby reached across the table and squeezed Brinn's hand. "I hope Bianca's able to help. I'm told she's a total pro."

"Thank you again," Brinn said. "I really appreciate your help."

"Any time. Now. Let's get into why I really invited you out." Her eyes danced with mischief.

"Ooookay," Brinn said slowly. "Why did you invite me here?"

"We're picking teams for our next golf cart race, and I want you on my cart this time. Wanda's been hogging you for far too long."

Brinn narrowed her eyes at Abby. "Why would you want me? My air magic isn't that impressive."

Abby shrugged one shoulder. "Maybe, maybe not, but you still have the ability to manipulate the wind, and that's always valuable. Regardless, I want you for your driving skills. No one knows Wanda better than you. We've got a high-stakes bet going on, and I *have* to beat her this time. I've thought long and hard about this, and I think you're the only one who can outdrive her."

"What's the bet?" Brinn asked, intrigued. Abby wasn't wrong. Brinn had been in countless golf cart races as Wanda's second. Brinn probably knew what moves Wanda would make even before she did. But she wasn't going to just sell her cousin out without a good reason.

Abby groaned. "She caught me in a sleep-deprivation haze and conned me into betting on our next race. If she wins, I not only have to detail her golf cart, but she's making me clean out that storage unit of hers. Have you seen it?"

Brinn shuddered. Wanda was the neatest person on the planet. Except for her secret storage unit she'd had for at least ten years. It's where she put everything she couldn't really use but couldn't bring herself to throw out either. It was packed to the rafters, and Brinn wouldn't be surprised if a few creatures hadn't moved in. It was so bad, Wanda hadn't even been in there for at least a few years. "That's awful, Abby. Please don't let her talk you into betting again until your kid is sleeping through the night."

Abby let out a sad laugh. "You're telling me. But if I win, she has to organize my inventory and set up a new ordering system to streamline my business." Abby sold magic-infused lotions, soaps, and energy drinks.

"You do realize she probably would've done that anyway, right?" Brinn said, shaking her head.

"Yes, but this way I won't have to feel guilty about it. Anyway, I just can't bear thinking about her storage unit. Would you please consider helping me?"

"Hook me up with a case of this beer and you have a deal," Brinn said, eyeing a spirit that had just appeared a few tables away.

"That's it?"

"That's it." Brinn got up. "Drop it off at Austin's. I've got to get going." The ghost was moving closer and had just made eye contact.

"You got it." Abby stood and followed her out. "But why Austin's?"

"I'm staying there for the moment," Brinn said, pulling out her keys.

"*Oh really*," Abby said, sounding gleeful. "How's that going?"

"Pretty good," Brinn said, unable to stop the soft smile from claiming her lips.

"I see." Abby nodded her approval. "Good for you."

"Thanks." Brinn got into her car just as the ghost joined them and started ranting about a bathroom remodel gone wrong.

"The shower tile was bad enough, but that toilet? It's what killed me. Have you ever had a toilet with so much suction that it literally pulled you in ass first?"

Brinn waved at Abby and slammed the door. A second later, she was speeding off toward Witches in Stitches as the ghost followed Abby back into the brewery. Brinn let out a sigh of relief, grateful that her friend was oblivious.

Only now Brinn wondered how long it would take for her to forget the idea of a woman dying by toilet suction. Would she suddenly form a phobia of toilets? She made a mental note to never flush while sitting.

Witches in Stitches was just a few blocks down, and when Brinn pulled into a spot right in front, she was surprised to see the store was dark. Though hadn't she just seen Zya at the vet earlier? Maybe she'd taken the day off. Brinn walked up to the door to check the store hours, and that's when she saw the sign.

Out of town. Closed until further notice.

CHAPTER 17

*a*ustin was elbow deep in a vat of melted chocolate when he heard the door open and shut. A reassuring calm washed over him. Brinn was back. Having her in his house made him content. Something he hadn't felt since he'd left Keating Hollow five years ago.

"What is happening here?" Brinn asked as she walked into the kitchen.

"Dessert." He pointed to *The Witch's Guide to Chocolate and Pastries*. "I was going to start with *Pain au Chocolate* until I realized it was going to take thirteen hours to prep the dough, so now we're having chocolate covered strawberries. Tomorrow I'll work on the *Pain au Chocolate*."

Brinn stared at him with the softest expression.

"What?" he asked, stirring the chocolate.

"You're incredible."

Austin's heart swelled with love for the amazing woman standing across the island from him. "Come here."

"Why?" she asked, giving him a flirty smile.

"I have something for you."

She looked him up and down, her gaze lingering on the chocolate. "Am I going to get a taste of that?"

"Absolutely."

"In that case…" Brinn moved until she was standing right next to Austin and stared down at the chocolate.

Austin picked up one of the strawberries he'd already prepared and slowly dipped it into the chocolate. He watched Brinn as her eyes followed his every movement. Holding the strawberry over the pot, they both watched as the excess chocolate dripped from the strawberry.

Drip. Drip. Drip.

"I think it's ready," Brinn said.

"You do?" He brought the strawberry up, moving it toward her mouth, but just as she opened to take a bite, Austin snatched it away and ate it himself.

"Hey!" she protested. "That was mean. You said I could taste the chocolate."

"I did, didn't I?" He dropped the rest of the strawberry onto the counter and then wrapped one arm around her waist and buried his other hand in her hair. With his mouth just inches from hers, he whispered, "Kiss me, Brinn."

"Oh," she breathed and grabbed his shirt as she brushed her lips over his. The moment he opened his mouth, she tasted him, moaning her approval.

Austin forgot everything, the strawberries, the chocolate, the lasagna baking in the oven, everything except the gorgeous woman in his arms. He tightened his hold, wishing he could keep her right there in his arms forever.

Brinn pulled back just enough to whisper, "Hmm, the chocolate is delicious."

"Then let me give you another taste."

She turned toward the pot of chocolate, eyeing it like a starving woman.

Austin laughed, dipped another strawberry, and this time when he brought it to her mouth, he watched hungrily as she wrapped her lips around it. "Damn, Brinn. You're killing me."

Her eyes lit with amusement, but as she watched him, they quickly turned heated. A moment later, she was pressed against him again, kissing him with everything she had.

Austin spun her around, pushing her up against the counter. The kiss went wild. Hands were everywhere. Skin. He needed to feel her skin-to-skin. He needed all of her. "Brinn, I—"

"Arf! Arf, arf!"

Brinn pulled away slightly and glanced over at Oz and Drusilla.

Austin let out a groan and followed her gaze. The two were sitting in the dog bed, staring intently at them. Oz seemed to be glaring at Austin, and his body was vibrating as if he was going to pounce at any moment.

"I think someone is feeling a little overprotective," Brinn said.

"He's protective of you," Austin groused as he took a step back.

Oz visibly relaxed, making Brinn laugh. "I think he thought you were attacking me," she said.

"I was. And if they hadn't interrupted, they were going to get quite the show." Austin stirred the chocolate, making sure the consistency was still good. When he was satisfied, he started dipping the rest of the strawberries. "Go check on your dogs," he told Brinn.

"*My dogs*?" she asked, sounding amused.

"They've claimed you. I don't think I have any say in the

matter." Did he sound bitter? Austin thought he sounded bitter.

"Aw, don't feel left out," she said as she reached down to pick up Dru. "At least Xander loves you." She nodded to the gray-striped cat who was sitting just to the right of him.

"He just wants a treat." Austin glanced down at the cat. "I'm onto you, buddy."

Brinn snorted. "That's probably true. But he loves you. I can tell."

Austin shook his head but didn't say anything as he watched the love of his life dote on Drusilla. After she thoroughly checked the bandage, loved on her, and coaxed her into swallowing her antibiotic, she carefully set the puppy back into the dog bed.

Oz sniffed the puppy, and when he was satisfied his new friend was okay, he turned to Brinn and jumped up, pawing at her shin.

"You, too?" Brinn asked before reaching down to pick him up. She let out a small groan. "Wow, bud. We might need to put you on a diet. Feels like you're getting a bit of a belly."

"Hey, now. Don't disparage my dog," Austin said. "Don't listen to her, Oz. The girls love that belly you have going on."

Brinn scratched his belly and laughed. "He's right, Oz. You're perfect just the way you are."

Was there anything better than this moment? Austin hadn't really ever seen himself as the domestic type, but standing there in his kitchen with dinner in the oven and dessert on the tray in front of him with Brinn and their combined brood of animals, he acknowledged that his priorities had changed. He was no longer content to just create music. He wanted this. Here in this house. With her.

"It smells wonderful in here," she said, pulling two wine glasses out of his cabinet.

"Your chef has been busy." He nodded to a bottle of wine he'd left on the counter. "Open the red."

She went to work on the cork and asked, "When did you learn to cook?"

Austin's grandmother had taught him the basics. He'd always been able to make a simple bowl of pasta with a jar of sauce or grill a steak. But putting together a lasagna or tempering chocolate had been well beyond his range before he'd moved out. "Money was tight when I left for LA. It was either learn to cook or keep eating canned soup every night."

"Well," she said, moving to stand next to him, "I have to say, you're pretty sexy working in the kitchen."

He smiled, loving flirty Brinn. While wiping the chocolate from his fingers, he took his time raking his gaze over her. "You're sexy all the time, but especially right now."

"Why right now?" she asked, holding his gaze.

"Because you're here. In my house. In my kitchen. Letting me cook for you."

She laughed. "Is that all it takes?"

"When it's you." He caressed her cheek with his thumb, chuckling when he smeared a line of chocolate. "Let me clean that up for you."

Brinn held still as he dipped his head and proceeded to kiss away the traces of chocolate he'd left on her skin. And when she sucked in a slight breath, he moved his head, kissing her again. Her lips were so soft, so eager. He desperately wanted to carry her up to his bedroom, but just when he was ready to sweep her up in his arms, the doorbell rang, bringing him back to reality as Oz jumped up, barking and running out of the room.

"Were we expecting company?" Brinn asked, breathless.

He let out a small groan. "Unfortunately. It's Gideon. He wanted to stop by to go over plans for the kids arts program. I ended up inviting him and Miranda for dinner. Is that okay?"

She stepped back, smoothing her shirt. "Uh, yeah. Just... I need a minute to freshen up."

"Sure. Take your time. I'll get the door." He followed her out of the kitchen and watched as she hurried upstairs. He stood there long enough that a knock sounded on the door, sending Oz into another fit of protectiveness. "It's okay, boy. They're expected." Austin patted Oz on the head and went to open the door. "Sorry to make you wait," he told his visitors. "I was caught up with something in the kitchen." It wasn't a total lie. He'd been completely caught up in what had been going on between him and Brinn.

"No problem," Gideon said, holding out a bottle of wine. "Thanks for the invite."

"Your house is gorgeous," Miranda said, peering around Austin. "I love the craftsman style."

"My grandmother was a big fan, too." Austin waved them into the foyer.

"Oh, look at this," Miranda said, making a beeline for the living room where Buffy, Xander, and Willow were all curled up together on the couch in a patch of sunlight. "Hello, beautiful babies." She sat on the ottoman and gave all three cats her full attention, scratching their ears and making kissing noises at them.

"She's a goner," Gideon said, shaking his head.

"Wait until she sees what we have waiting for her in the kitchen," Austin said with a chuckle.

Austin eyed the satchel Gideon was carrying. "You can put that here for now." He pointed to the bench near the front door. "Dinner's almost ready. I thought we'd eat first, then get down to business."

"Sounds good to me."

After Gideon stored his bag, the two men made their way into the kitchen. As soon as Gideon spotted Drusilla, he groaned." Oh no. Miranda is going to go supersonic when she sees that."

"Everyone does," Austin said as he pulled the lasagna out of the oven. He placed it on the stove to set up and was just about to set the table when the highest-pitched squeal he'd ever heard pierced his brain. "Holy hell," he muttered.

"I told you," Gideon muttered back.

"Look at this sweet baby. Oh. Em. Gee. I've never seen anything cuter." Miranda sat right on the floor next to the dog bed and leaned down to give both Dru and Oz kisses. Oz moved to press his entire body against her leg and then rolled over, showing her his belly.

"Would you look at that? No loyalty at all," Austin said, shaking his head.

"These babies are precious, Austin," Miranda said. "It's just not fair to have this much cuteness all at once."

"Right?" Brinn said as she strolled in, her hair done up in a bun with tendrils falling loosely around her face.

Austin's breath caught. She just got more beautiful every time he saw her.

"Hey, Brinn," Miranda said, standing to greet her. "I *love* your new puppy."

The two women spent the next ten minutes fussing over the puppy and Oz until Austin said, "Dinner's on the table."

"We're coming. Keep your pants on," Miranda said.

After washing up, the four sat at the table, where there was lasagna, salad, and garlic bread waiting.

"Did you do all this?" Gideon asked him.

Austin shrugged.

"He did," Brinn said, beaming. "He made the chocolate covered strawberries, too."

"He's a keeper," Miranda said.

"I know." Brinn met Austin's gaze. The love shining back at him touched him right to the core.

Home.

This is what home felt like.

And he was here to stay.

CHAPTER 18

*B*rinn sat at the table, more content than she'd ever been. Dinner had been excellent, and the company even better. Gideon was a kind man, and obviously in love with Miranda. The way they were with each other, finishing each other's sentences, attentive and teasing. Their relationship was one for the books.

Austin stood and reached for the dishes to clear the table.

"Oh, no. You cooked," Brinn said, getting to her feet. "I've got this."

"It's no problem," Austin assured her.

"Nope. The cook does not clean." She gently nudged him back into the chair. "It's only fair."

Brinn started clearing the table, and Miranda quickly joined her while the two men got to work on planning their art program.

"Looks like things are going really well between the two of you," Miranda whispered.

"They are." Brinn watched the two men, their heads together as they worked out the logistics of their program.

"He's exactly the same man he was five years ago, only better somehow. And I…" She sucked in a breath. "I don't know what I'll do if he leaves again."

Miranda let out a soft chuckle. "Honey, that man isn't going anywhere."

"You don't know that." As much as Brinn wanted to believe Austin was staying put, she knew he'd built a life somewhere else. It wasn't fair to ask him to give it up for her… especially since they'd barely restarted their relationship.

"Yeah. I do." She winked at Brinn and reached over to squeeze her hand. "Sometimes, I just know things."

Brinn eyed the writer. "You always say that, but how do I know it's true?"

"Trust, Brinn. Trust." She poured herself another glass of wine, smirked, and then went to sit next to Gideon.

Brinn stood at the counter watching Austin. He waved his arms as he talked animatedly about the music program he wanted to implement. And when Gideon suggested they rope Chad Garber, the owner of Magical Notes, into teaching a few classes, Austin's eyes lit up. He was enjoying every moment with Gideon.

He'd found a kindred spirit who was just as passionate about the project as he was. Brinn peered closer, noticing something she hadn't expected to see. There was something about the pair that was just familiar. Like the fact that each of their left eyebrows had the same curve. They both used the same half-smile when they were trying to convince the other one of a new idea. But the most interesting thing was that they both had the same build. She hadn't noticed it before, but having them side by side, it was hard not to see the similarities. If she didn't know better, she'd think they were brothers or cousins or something.

Brinn chuckled at herself. That was impossible. Austin didn't have any siblings and neither did his father. She wasn't sure about his mother, but Austin hadn't ever spoken of relatives besides his immediate family.

A flash of movement from the other side of the room caught Brinn's attention. When she spotted the ghost, her heart and her stomach both sank. Not now! Couldn't she just have one night off? Apparently, that was a negative. But why was the ghost in the house? While she'd seen a couple on the property, this was the first she'd witnessed inside the house.

Brinn intended to ignore the ghost completely, but when the ghost turned her head slightly, the woman was none other than Peggy Steele, Austin's grandmother. Brinn wanted to ask her what she was doing there, but she wouldn't in front of Miranda and Gideon. While Brinn assumed they'd both heard about her recent problem through the gossip grapevine and knew she had the gift to see spirits, it wasn't something she wanted to talk about at all.

But it appeared Peggy didn't want to do any talking either. As Brinn got closer, she noted that Peggy had been watching her grandson with a tender expression and was dabbing at her eyes.

Because it was Peggy, Brinn abandoned her decision to stay far away from ghosts. If she could get information out of Austin's grandmother, she had to try. But before she could get close enough to speak to her, Peggy took one last glance at both Austin and Gideon, smiled softly, and then faded away.

"Brinn," Austin said. "Come sit with us. The kitchen's as clean as it's going to get. Don't you think?"

She nodded, grabbed the tray of chocolate covered strawberries, and sat down next to Austin.

"You're a goddess," he said and took a strawberry.

Neither Gideon nor Miranda were shy about trying the strawberries. It wasn't long before the tray was empty and the work had been put aside. They spent the next two hours, talking, laughing, and catching up on the latest Keating Hollow gossip.

By the time Brinn and Austin walked their guests to the door, Brinn's batteries had been more than charged. She was practically floating on happiness.

When Austin shut the door, he turned to her. "You look like you had a good time."

"So do you," she said, stepping in closer and pressing her hands to his chest.

"I did. It's hard to understand why my grandmother left money to Gideon, but she obviously knew what she was doing. Who could've predicted that we'd form a nonprofit together and also become friends?"

"That's a question above my pay grade," Brinn said softly. "What I'm wondering is if we're going to take this party upstairs."

Silence hung in the air around them for a few beats as Austin stared down at her.

Her skin started to prickle with anxiety, but when Austin nodded slowly, all her nerves vanished. This was it. This was the moment when she put their past behind them and started to trust that maybe they could be together. That this time would be different. She knew that thought should scare her. People repeated their mistakes more often than not when it came to matters of the heart. But Brinn was ready to risk it all if that meant she had Austin back in her life.

Austin held out his hand to her. "Ready?"

"Yes."

They took a moment to check on the animals, and then

Austin slipped his arm around Brinn's waist and led her upstairs. But instead of walking her to her door, he steered her down the hall to his bedroom.

Brinn glanced around at the large room before her eyes landed on the giant king-size bed. The bed was cloaked in a thick black comforter and accented with pure white pillows. No color anywhere.

"Are you okay?" Austin stood just to the side of Brinn, clutching at her waist.

"No. I don't think so," Brinn said nervously. But no matter how anxious she was, she was not leaving Austin's bedroom. She'd made up her mind, and tonight was the night. She smiled up at him. "But don't let that stop you."

"Brinn," he whispered and brushed back her hair. "You know nothing's going to happen if—*oomph*."

No more talking. That's all that had run through Brinn's brain before she launched herself at Austin. She'd waited five long years to be back in his arms. Nerves or no nerves, she wasn't waiting any longer. After a long, satisfying kiss, she broke their connection just long enough to say, "I want you, and I want this. Understand?"

He nodded, his lips already finding her jawline and heading south to the base of her neck.

Brinn craned her neck, giving him better access. And just like that, there wasn't any more conversation between the two of them. They let their lips, hands, and bodies do the talking for them. Over and over and over again.

BRINN WAS DREAMING she was a cat and was lying on the floor in a patch of sun. She felt languid and satisfied and achy in the best possible way.

"Good morning," a deep voice said into her ear.

"Hmmm," Brinn reached up, stretching and then settling again as she tilted her head toward the sun. There was no reason to get up. She was a cat. What else did she have to do that day?

But then warm kisses teased her skin and Brinn opened one eye. The most handsome man she'd ever seen was hovering over her, shirtless, as he rained kisses down on her bare skin.

"Not a cat," she said, running her hand through his gorgeous curls.

He paused the kissing and looked up at her. "Did you just call me a cat?"

"No." She shook her head, trying not to laugh. "I was dreaming I was a cat lying contentedly in the sun. I didn't want to move."

"Content? Is that the best you have after the night we had together?"

"No. Not at all. Satisfying, fun, sexy… Are those better words?" she asked.

"Yes, much." Austin continued his exploration of Brinn's body until she was panting with need. He lifted his gaze to stare her in the eye and said, "I want you, Brinn. One night wasn't enough."

She nodded fiercely. "I want you, too."

"Thank the gods," he whispered. And then he took his time worshipping her one more time before he had to start his day.

An hour later, Brinn lay in the bed naked with just the sheet covering her. Austin had already gotten up and had run out to pick up some coffee and pastries from Incantation Café. Brinn was all too happy to luxuriate in his bed. The night before and that morning had been... incredible. Better and more intense than it had ever been between them. Austin had been tender and loving and then in other moments, rough and demanding. Her body was still tingling from the pleasure. It seemed a shame to get up and shower. If she had her way, she'd stay in bed all day, preferably with Austin. But they both had work to do.

She glanced at the clock and groaned. If she didn't get up and get ready soon, she wouldn't have any time for breakfast with Austin. She rolled out of Austin's bed, made it up, and then hurried toward the shower, completely naked.

Brinn felt slightly exposed walking along the upstairs hallway. She could have used Austin's shower, but all of her toiletries were already lined up in the guest bathroom. Would he mind if she moved them into his bathroom? Judging by the activities of the last twelve hours, she figured he probably wouldn't mind.

When Brinn emerged from the shower, she chuckled at herself when she realized she'd forgotten her robe. And she only had one clean towel. Her options were to leave her hair dripping and cover up, or wrap her hair in the towel and just walk naked to her room. She chose to be naked. Why not? The only person who would be there was Austin. It wasn't as if she hadn't proved she was more than willing to bare herself to him.

She'd just stepped out of the bathroom when she heard Austin clear his throat. She turned, intending to say something flirty when her words faded away at the sight of the man standing just feet from her. He wasn't Austin at all. Instead, he was someone who was about twenty-five years older and had the same facial features.

Mathew Steele. She'd never officially met him before, but she'd seen him around town and knew who he was. Everyone had.

Austin's dad had his arms crossed over his chest and he was staring at her as if she'd just committed a crime. In her birthday suit. "Holy hell!" she cried and ran into her bedroom, slamming the door behind her. Where had he come from? Was Austin even home yet? Her face flamed with embarrassment.

Twenty minutes later when Brinn finally poked her head out of the door, the hallway was empty, and she let out a sigh of relief. Maybe she could sneak out of the house before she ran into Austin's dad again. She pulled out her phone and texted Austin. *Where are you?*

There was no immediate reply.

Damn. She contemplated making a run for it, but she needed to feed the cats and check on Dru. Sucking in a calming breath, she held her head up high and made her way downstairs to the kitchen.

Oz came running up to her, while Dru sat in the dog bed, wagging her tail. It wasn't long before the cats started slinking in. She got them all situated, gave them kisses, and then made a beeline for the door. She'd talk to Austin later.

Just as Brinn reached for the door, she spotted movement to her left.

"Brinn Taylor, right?"

She nodded, not sure what to say to the man after the incident upstairs. *Sorry I flashed you my goods* didn't seem appropriate.

"Well, this is an awkward way to officially meet for the first time. I certainly wasn't expecting to find you in my mother's house this morning. Was there a reason you were walking around naked like you owned the place?"

Son of a... Brinn swallowed her anger at the man. She hadn't forgotten what Austin had said about his threats against her grandmother's café. But for Austin's sake, she was trying to let it go. "My apologies, Mr. Steele. I had no idea anyone else was here. Have you seen Austin?"

"No. He wasn't here when I arrived." He slowly walked over to her. When he was only a foot away, he looked her up and down, a snarl on his lips as he said, "You shouldn't be here."

"Why? Your son invited me," she said, anger starting to churn in her gut. "He obviously wants me here."

"He doesn't know what he wants. Trust me, it's better for you both if you just move on now."

"I'm not *moving on*," she said, standing toe-to-toe with him. "My relationship with Austin doesn't concern you."

The door suddenly swung open, and Austin came to an abrupt stop when he spotted Brinn and his father staring each other down. He set the coffee cup tray and pastry bag on the bench beside the door as he asked, "Dad? What's going on? When did you get here?"

"About a half hour ago." He turned his judgmental stare on his son. "Imagine my surprise when I stumbled upon a naked woman making herself at home in my mother's house."

"Naked?" Austin asked, frowning. "Brinn was wandering around naked?"

"I wasn't wandering around," Brinn said exasperated. "I was walking from the bathroom to the guest room. I had no idea he was there."

Austin moved to Brinn's side and took her hand. Some of the tension fled Brinn's body. She hadn't realized just how much she'd needed his support.

"Dad, stop being so hostile. I'm allowed to have visitors in my own house," Austin said, closing the door behind him.

"My mother's house," he insisted. "I very much doubt she would approve of this one." He nodded toward Brinn.

"What?" Austin's body stiffened and his grip tightened around her hand. "Gran loved Brinn. Besides. It's not her call anyway. Or yours."

Mathew Steele shook his head, seemingly disappointed. "Can't you see it, son? She's using you. For your money. It didn't take her anytime at all to move herself right in after your grandmother passed, did it?"

"*She's* using me?" Austin said, exasperated. "Stop now, Dad, before you embarrass yourself."

Mathew rolled his shoulders as if trying to force himself to relax. "Maybe we should talk about this in private."

Brinn let out an irritated huff. "I'd prefer to stay if you're going to be insulting me, Mr. Steele."

He narrowed his eyes at her. "This conversation is between me and my son."

Austin snorted. "This conversation is over. Brinn is staying here, and that's all there is to say about it. You can either apologize for being a massive A-hole and get over it, or you can leave."

Brinn squeezed Austin's hand, silently thanking him for standing up for her. He squeezed back but never took his gaze from his father.

Mathew looked between them, shook his head, and then turned around, disappearing into the office.

Austin muttered a curse before turning to Brinn. "I'm sorry about that. I forgot he was coming today. Or maybe I just put it out of my mind. Still, I had no idea he was going to go Full Metal Asshole like that on you. What the hell is his problem?"

"He thinks I'm a gold digger," Brinn said. "I guess it's his messed-up way of protecting you."

"I don't need his protection." He cupped one of her cheeks and stared down at her. "I really am sorry. You didn't deserve any of that. Will you come back after work?"

She bit her bottom lip, not sure what to say. She wanted to be near Austin for obvious reasons, but if his dad was going to be that hostile, she couldn't keep subjecting herself to that. Closing her eyes, she sighed. "I guess I'll have to even if I don't stay. The cats and Dru are here."

Austin leaned down and kissed her cheek. "He'll either have to behave himself, or I'll make it clear he's not welcome here."

"You'd throw your own dad out for me?" she asked, her eyes going wide.

"Brinn, there's nothing I wouldn't do for you."

CHAPTER 19

uming, Austin dumped his coffee down the sink and tried to get a grip on himself. He couldn't believe what he'd just walked in on. How dare his father walk in and accuse Brinn of using him for his money? Money that he was giving away, no less. His father had no idea what he was talking about.

When Austin had calmed down enough that he no longer wanted to deck his father, he calmly walked through the house to his office. The door was still closed, and he didn't bother knocking. It was *his* office after all.

Austin swung the door open and walked in. Just seeing his father sitting behind his desk, going through his paperwork, lit him up again. "What are you doing?"

"What is this?" He held up a manilla folder. The one that had to be his grandmother's trust.

"Exactly what it looks like," Austin said. "Why are you rummaging around in my desk?" It was a petty question. The folder had been sitting on the desk just as it had been since he'd dug it out after his grandmother passed.

His father threw the paperwork back down on the desk. "What are you doing about it?"

"About what, exactly? The estate is almost settled. There isn't much more to do." He took a few steps closer, narrowing his eyes at his father. "More importantly, why did you come in here and insult Brinn for no reason? I won't tolerate you talking about her like that."

"Dammit, Austin!" he thundered as he smacked his fist down on the banker's desk. "You're too naive for your own good. Can't you see these people are taking advantage of you? That this Gideon person must've found a way to get himself written into her will? You have to contest it. If you don't, I will."

Austin straightened his shoulders and, with an air of superiority he hadn't realized he possessed, said, "You will do no such thing. Brinn isn't using me. If you say that again, this relationship you've pushed so hard to try to rebuild is over. Do you understand?"

A muscle twitched in his father's jaw, and Austin knew he was struggling to keep whatever he really wanted to say to himself. "You're a grown man. I guess you'll just have to learn from your own mistakes."

"You'd know all about that, wouldn't you, Dad?" The barb just flew out of his mouth. It definitely wouldn't help repair anything between them, but it felt good in the moment. He wasn't letting his father try to run his life. Not this time. Not ever again.

"Yes, I do. And don't think I haven't paid for them. I'm just trying to keep you from going down that same road."

"You don't have to worry about that," Austin said. "I don't keep booze in a flask on my person. By the way, I already checked out Gideon Alexander. He's a decent man who had no idea he was named in her will. He even tried to decline the inheritance. So let that go. It was Gran's choice to leave him part of her estate. We will respect her wishes."

"Austin," his father growled. "You're pushing me."

"Oh, I'm sorry. Was I supposed to be respectful after you were rude to Brinn and implied that I'm lacking sound judgment on how to live my life when all signs point to the fact that I have everything under control?"

"You don't have everything under control!" his father thundered. "You managed to lose half your grandmother's net worth to some stranger, and you've gotten involved with a woman who is beneath you!"

Austin's blood ran cold. His father's words shook him to his very core. That threat he'd made all those years ago to ruin Brinn's grandmother's business hadn't been entirely about getting Austin to work with his dad. Mathew Steele was a pretentious snob who didn't want his son with a townie. "I think it's time for you to leave," Austin said, his tone clipped and full of ice. "You've already outstayed your welcome."

"This is my mother's house," his father said with an air of authority. "I don't think you'll kick me out today."

"Oh, you don't?" Austin scoffed. "This is my house now. The deed has already been transferred. That's the good thing about trusts; they don't hold things up. If you don't leave, I'll call the sheriff and have you removed. Understand?"

"Don't be ridiculous, Austin," Mathew said. "You're not going to call the sheriff on your father." He sat down in the office chair and reached for the landline phone. "Now, either get on board or don't. But I'm calling my lawyer. I won't let this Gideon person take her money without a fight."

Austin pulled his phone out of his pocket. After finding the sheriff office's number, he made the call and put it on speaker.

"Keating Hollow Sheriff's office," the receptionist said. "Clarissa speaking."

"Hey, Clarissa. This is Austin Steele. Is Deputy Sheriff Baker available?"

"Is this an emergency?" she asked.

"No. Just a trespassing case. I need someone, preferably Drew, to come escort him off my property."

"I'll put you right through," she said.

"Austin, hang up that phone. This is completely unnecessary," his father said, not bothering to hide his exasperation.

"I see what you mean," Clarissa said.

"I thought you were transferring him to the sheriff?" Mathew barked.

"Oh, I am, sir. But I'm listening in until he picks up. Protocol," she said.

Austin chuckled. Sure it was. He got the feeling that Clarissa knew everything that went on in Keating Hollow and this was one of the reasons why.

"This is ridiculous," Mathew said. "I'm not leaving this house."

"Baker here," Drew said over the line. "Did Clarissa say this is about a trespassing?"

"Yes," Austin said at the same time as his father said, "No."

"Domestic dispute?" Drew asked.

"It could certainly turn into one," Austin said. "I've asked my father to leave, and he's refusing. Can you send someone to escort him out?"

"It's my mother's house!" Mathew bellowed.

"It *was* your mother's house. It's mine now," Austin said, running out of patience.

"It sounds like maybe you should pack it in, sir," Drew said mildly. "I'm sure everyone could use a little time to cool off."

"I'm fine," Mathew barked, sounding anything but fine.

"I see. Well then, I guess I'll see you folks in a few minutes." The line went dead and Austin put his phone back in his pocket. Without another word, he spun and left the room.

"Austin!" his father called.

Austin gritted his teeth, vowing to ignore him. He should have known better than to agree to letting his father stay in his grandmother's house. But he supposed the fact that it had been her house was why Austin hadn't felt like he could say no.

His father's heavy footsteps rang through the house as he followed Austin toward the kitchen. "Call the deputy back. Tell him he isn't needed."

"No."

"You're being insolent."

Austin shrugged. "If you say so."

"Dammit. Why are you so stubborn?"

That was enough. Austin was done. He'd been down this road with his father before. Mathew Steele wasn't going to give up until he got what he wanted. There was no use in fighting with him. His father always had to have the last word.

"Answer me!" his father demanded.

Oz came running into the room, his high-pitched barking ringing through the house.

"That's enough, Oz!" Mathew ordered.

The barking continued, making Mathew yell even louder. Oz ignored him.

Austin snapped his fingers. "Enough." Oz stopped instantly and trotted over to Austin's side.

"I guess he knows who his master is," Mathew muttered and stormed out of the room.

"Good job, Oz," Austin said. "You're the only one who's managed to get him to leave when he wasn't wanted."

Oz wagged his tail and stared up at Austin in adoration.

Austin reached down and picked up his dog. He scratched his ears, told him he was a good boy, and walked into the living room where Dru was busy chewing on an unfamiliar shoe. He put Oz down and took the shoe from the puppy. When he saw the brand and the size, he started to laugh.

How his father had already managed to lose one of his shoes to a three-pound shih tzu, he'd never know. But karma was in full force and he was here for it.

Austin started to move back to his office, but the sound of footsteps on the stairs stopped him. He looked up and spotted his father making his way down with two suitcases in hand.

Mathew paused at the bottom of the landing, glanced at his son, and said, "I'm contesting the trust. My lawyer is already working on it."

Austin scowled but said nothing. When the door slammed behind his father, he moved to the window. Deputy Sheriff Baker had just parked and was climbing out of his car. The two men exchanged a few words before Mathew got into his car and left. When Austin could no longer see his father's taillights, he opened the door to greet Drew.

"Looks like your father decided to leave on his own," the deputy said.

Austin's lips twitched. "I guess when faced with the long arm of the law, he decided not to fight."

"That happens."

"I'm sorry you had to come all the way out here for nothing," Austin said. "But I appreciate it."

"It wasn't for nothing. It never is." Drew tipped his hat and retreated to his SUV.

Austin pulled his phone out again and called Gideon.

"Hey, partner. How's it going? Did you think of something else to add to the plan?" Gideon asked.

"Nothing more for the plan at the moment. But I do have a warning for you. Something you need to be aware of." Austin sat in one of the armchairs that looked out into the woods on his property. "My father was here. He's on a rampage and wants to contest the trust."

"Let me guess. He's not happy some stranger is getting his share of the estate?" Gideon asked.

"He seemed fine with it when he thought I was getting it all. When he found out you're a beneficiary, that's when he lost it."

"Okay. Well, you know my stance on this," Gideon said. "I don't need the money. I won't fight this. You can have the money and still fund the kids arts program."

"That would be fine, but I don't think for a minute that he's going to fight for me to get it all," Austin said, already knowing that his father had found an opening and wanted a bigger piece of the pie. "He's going to say he has a claim, and I can't let that happen. So I'm asking you, please, don't give up this fight."

"Can I ask why?"

"Two reasons," Austin said. "The first is that my grandmother made her wishes clear. She didn't want him to have a large portion of her estate. The second is because he's an ass and I won't give him the satisfaction."

Gideon let out a quiet chuckle. "Understood. I'll inform my lawyer to be on the lookout."

Austin let out a sigh of relief. He hadn't until that very moment realized just how angry he was with his father. Maybe it was petty revenge, but he was willing to do just about anything to keep his father from stealing that inheritance.

CHAPTER 20

"How many coffee cakes have you had today?" Yvette asked. She was sitting at one of the bookstore's café tables, working on her laptop.

"This is the fourth." Brinn wiped the excess crumbs from her lips and pressed one hand against her belly.

"Stomachache?" Yvette asked.

"Just a little." Brinn rushed over to the counter to help a few customers check out, and when she returned to the café, she flopped down in the chair across from Yvette.

"What happened?" Yvette didn't take her gaze off her laptop screen as she continued to type.

"Austin's dad saw me naked this morning," Brinn blurted.

"What?" Yvette closed her laptop and gave Brinn her undivided attention.

"You heard me. I was just going across the hall, and he was just right there."

Yvette laughed. "Oh no. What did you do?"

"I ran. Obviously." Brinn gave her a you-can't-be-serious look. "What else was I supposed to do?"

"I don't know," Yvette said slowly. "I've never been in that position. Though Wanda has. You should ask her about it sometime. Something about waiting in Cameron's bed only to have his parents walk in. I heard it was quite the show."

"You're joking, right?" Brinn asked, unable to stop the surprised burst of laughter from bubbling up.

"Nope." She drew a cross on her chest with her finger. "That really happened, and look at them now."

"I can't believe she never told me that." Brinn shook her head.

"Are you going to tell her about Austin's dad?"

"Not if I can help it."

"So…" Yvette said carefully. "You were at Austin's? Naked?"

Brinn's face heated, and she was sure she'd turned bright red. "I was going from the bathroom to the guest room."

"Uh-huh. Are you trying to tell me you slept alone last night?"

"That's not… I didn't…" Brinn stammered.

Yvette laughed. "I just hope it was Austin who kept you warm last night and not his father."

"Oh my god. You did not just suggest I would ever do anything with Mathew Steele." She visibly shuddered. "Even if he wasn't more than twenty-five years my senior, he's the last person I'd let put his hands on me. The pompous ass."

"That good, huh?"

"He's the worst," Brinn said.

A ghost materialized right beside Yvette with one hand on her hip and the other one pointing at Brinn. "He can't be worse than my husband. The gold-digging, cheating deadbeat."

"Go away," Brinn said to the ghost.

"Uh, okay," Yvette said, already grabbing her laptop.

"Not you." Brinn nodded to the space beside her. "I'm

talking to the bitter ghost who's complaining about her husband."

"I'm not bitter!" the ghost screamed. "I'm pissed. That bastard wrecked my car and stole the money out of my daughter's account the day after I died. I need you to go kick his ass!"

Brinn stared at the weatherworn woman. She looked like she'd spent the majority of her summers covered in baby oil by the pool. Probably with one of those silver reflectors. She'd be the perfect poster child for warnings against sun damage.

"Is she agitated?" Yvette asked.

"Yes." Brinn nodded. "How did you know?"

"The energy in here just got really... I don't know, uncomfortable."

"You're uncomfortable?" the ghost scoffed. "Try being dead. See where that gets you. Or having to walk around with a gaping wound in your head." She turned, showing off her blood-matted hair. "Cause of death, blunt trauma."

Brinn groaned and covered her face with her hands. "When will this stop?"

"You're going to have to be more specific," Yvette said. "The ghosts or dealing with Austin's dad?"

Brinn groaned louder. How was she going to walk back into Austin's house knowing that Mathew Steele was going to be there? The very idea made her want to punch something. Preferably Mathew Steele. As far as she knew, no one else deserved it.

"That didn't exactly clear things up," Yvette said.

"The ghosts. They're driving me insane." She glanced up and glared at the ghost who was still hovering nearby.

"Oh, please," the ghost said, sounding disgusted. "I'm the

one who's dead. Imagine how that feels." The ghost walked off in a huff, gliding right through the front door.

"Did you call that medium that Abby found for you?"

Only vaguely relieved, Brinn peered at her boss. "How did you know about that?"

"Please. Abby's my sister. What else are we going to talk about at family dinners?"

Brinn got up and headed to the coffee bar. "You know what we need? Irish Whiskey. That would really bring the customers in."

"Put it in the suggestion box." Yvette opened her laptop again, but before she got to work, she said, "I noticed you didn't answer my question about the medium."

"You're quick," Brinn quipped.

"Call her. Figure out how to get a handle on this thing before they use up all your energy and turn you into a rambling idiot."

"That's a pretty picture," Brinn mumbled as she made herself a latte.

"Make me one, too," Yvette said.

"On it."

Once the lattes were done and Yvette got back to work on her computer, Brinn took her seat behind the front counter. It was late afternoon, the time of day when the shop was normally quiet. But today, the silence was almost deafening. She pulled out the number Abby had given her and finally made the call.

"Bianca Blue," the woman on the other end of the call said.

"Uh, hi, Bianca. This is Brinn Taylor—"

"Oh, Abby's friend. I've been expecting you." Bianca's cheerfulness surprised Brinn. She wasn't sure why, except maybe because the ghosts were exhausting her and she found it hard to believe anyone would choose to talk to ghosts for a living.

"Right. Well, I was hoping to get some advice."

"Sure. You're a medium, too, right?"

Brinn nodded even though the woman couldn't see her. "Yes. But this is sort of new to me, and I'm hoping you can give me some tips on how to control it. How do you keep the spirits from flocking to you at all times?"

"Spirits flock to you?" she asked, sounding a little bit surprised.

"Yes. I mean, they aren't around all the time, but they show up regularly and start demanding that I take care of their unfinished business. It's every day, and I can't seem to be able to block them out or keep any sort of barriers for my mental health."

"Hmm."

What did that mean? "Bianca?" Brinn asked after a long silence.

"I'm here. I'm just not sure how I can help you. It's not like that for me. I have to perform rituals to open myself up to the spirits."

"What, like using a Ouija board?" Brinn asked, horrified. She'd never touch one of those in a million years.

"That would be one way, yes. But I prefer herb offerings. I hold the ritual each morning before I open for business."

Brinn shuddered. "So you're literally welcoming them in?"

"Yeah." The woman's voice had lost its cheerfulness, and now she sounded contemplative. "But at the end of the day, I do another ritual to close that door. Maybe that will help you?"

Brinn perked up. Now that sounded promising. "Yes. That sounds like a great idea. Would you mind sharing your ritual?"

"Not at all. Do you have a pen and paper?"

"I'm ready," Brinn said and then scribbled down the herbs needed and the incantation. It was a fairly simple spell that clearly worked off intensions, and Brinn found herself doubting that it would work for her. Still, she was willing to try it. She was willing to try *anything* in order to be freed of listening to ghosts who wanted her to do their bidding. After she reread the instructions and Bianca confirmed she had everything correct, Brinn said, "Thank you, Bianca. I really appreciate it."

"You're welcome." She paused for a moment before speaking again. "You know, if you wanted to embrace this gift, you'd make a killing. I've only met one other medium who didn't have to do anything in order to regularly communicate with spirits, and she was in very high demand. She was able to command top dollar, too. In just a year, she went from renting a room with four other roommates to owning her own French Quarter condo."

"That's… impressive." Brinn didn't know what else to say. This wasn't about money for her. She had a house and a job she liked. She didn't *need* more money. What she needed was some peace. Though maybe talking to her would be helpful. "You wouldn't happen to have her number, would you? I'd love to ask her how she handles everything."

There was silence on the other end of the line.

"Bianca?" she asked.

"Oh, sorry. I'm here. Trixie passed away a few years ago."

Brinn felt sick. Deep in her gut, she just knew that whatever had happened to Trixie, it was related to her communicating with the dead. "Do I want to know what happened?"

"No," Bianca said, sounding sad. "It was such a tragedy. I told her to leave that case alone, but she didn't listen."

"I see. I'm sorry to hear that," Brinn said as a wave of sadness hit her for the woman she'd never met. "Thank you for your time. I appreciate it."

"Sure, Brinn. And feel free to call anytime if you have any more questions or even if you just want to talk. I'm always open to new friends, especially other mediums."

"Thanks. That's very kind. I'll be in touch." Brinn ended the call, not sure if she'd meant it when she said she'd keep in touch with the other woman. It sounded like their life experiences were completely opposite.

"Not what you wanted to hear, was it?"

Brinn spun around and spotted a tall, slender ghost dressed in a black lace corset dress. Her hair fell in soft curls around her face. Her wide eyes and pouty lips made her look like she belonged on the cover of a magazine. "Who are you?"

"The spirit who was sent to watch over you," she said, eyeing Brinn up and down. "You'll never make it."

"What?" Brinn asked, but the ghost was already gone. Anger curled up from her belly, making her want to scream. The phone call was supposed to help. Only now she was certain that talking to another medium had only made things worse.

Brinn stalked away from the counter, bypassed the pastry bar, and walked into the back room. With a box cutter in hand, she tore into the deliveries that had been left that morning and did her best to work out her frustrations with physical labor.

"Is that helping?" a familiar voice said from the doorway.

Brinn slashed another box. While pulling the books out, she glanced up at her cousin. "No. Not at all."

Wanda gave her a sympathetic smile and walked in. Without saying a word, she wrapped her arms around Brinn and hugged her.

Brinn stood there, frozen for a moment before returning

the embrace. Tears pricked her eyes, but it wasn't because of the ghosts that kept plaguing her. It was because Wanda was here. Because Yvette had obviously called in reinforcement. Brinn didn't have a lot of people in her life who she was close to. Sure, she had friends. The Townsend sisters, Miranda, and some of the other women in town were friendly. But she didn't have a best friend. Wanda was the closest thing to that. But growing up, Wanda had been best friends with Abby. It hadn't left a lot of room for Brinn, who was a few years younger.

"You okay?" Wanda asked.

"Yeah. Just exhausted, and I'm not sure where I'm sleeping tonight." She put the box cutter down and leaned against the wall.

Wanda raised an eyebrow. "Not at your house?"

Brinn shrugged. "Maybe. I spent last night with... at Austin's."

"Which is it? *With* or *at?*" Wanda asked, eyeing her with curiosity.

"Both?" Brinn admitted. "For some reason when I'm at his house, ghosts don't bother me. So he let me stay and..." She cleared her throat. "You know."

Wanda grinned. "I don't know. But I will if you tell me. How was it? Are you going to do it again? Has he gotten better with age?"

Brinn couldn't help chuckling. Leave it to Wanda to coax her out of her maudlin mood. "How about I just say that it was a good night and leave it at that."

"You're no fun," she pouted. But then she narrowed her eyes and asked, "So if you had a great night, why wouldn't you go back tonight? You're not running from him, are you? Listen, Brinn—"

Brinn held her hand up. "You don't have to say it. I know

Austin deserves another chance. It's not that. I want to go back, but his dad is in town and he was a major ass this morning. I can't stay in the same house with that man. Which means I'll need to pick up the cats and head home. I just… His dad was the reason our relationship went south last time. If he gets between us again…" Brinn shook her head. "I hate this."

"I know." Wanda took her hand. "It's quitting time, right?" When Brinn nodded, Wanda said, "Good. Come with me. I think I know something that might help."

"What?" Brinn asked.

"You'll see."

CHAPTER 21

"*H*op in," Wanda said, gesturing to her sparkling purple, tricked-out golf cart.

Brinn eyed the cooler in the back. "You're not going to offer me a drink?"

"I was going to wait until we reached our destination, but if you're desperate—"

"I am desperate," Brinn said and helped herself to an ice-cold beer. It had a Keating Hollow Brewery label, and after the day Brinn had, it tasted like heaven.

"Feel better?" Wanda asked as she pulled out of the parking space in front of Hollow Books.

"I will when I've had a couple of these."

Wanda chuckled. "Good thing I just restocked."

"You know what we need?" Brinn tightened her jacket around herself as the wind picked up.

"What's that?"

"Snacks. We need all the snacks."

"On it." Wanda zipped into a parking spot right in front of Incantation Café. "Be right back." When she returned, she handed Brinn a bag of cookies and two mocha lattes. "Ready now?"

Brinn took a bite of the snickerdoodle and muttered, "Yes."

"Enjoy your sugar coma," Wanda teased and then flipped on the music. P!nk started singing about getting the party started while the lights on the golf cart flashed to the beat.

"You know what you need?" Brinn asked.

"What's that?"

"Heated seats. Now that's something to get excited about."

Wanda gave her an approving glance. "Now that's brilliant."

"It comes naturally." Brinn bobbed her shoulders along to the beat and couldn't deny that she felt better already. Wanda had a special ability to bring joy into the world, and tonight, she was delivering on that reputation.

It wasn't long before Wanda turned onto the path that led down to the magical river that ran through town. The moon was shining bright, lighting up the water and the open space where they usually had their golf cart races. But instead of heading down to the river like they usually did, Wanda turned on the headlights and made a turn into the trees onto a dirt road. It was smooth sailing for a about a mile, but when she navigated onto another path through the redwoods, it turned bumpy.

"Where are we going?" Brinn asked.

"You'll see."

Brinn eyed her for a moment before giving her full attention to the forest. "It seems like we're taking the scenic route to your house. Isn't it in this direction?"

"Yes, but we're not going to the house. There's something else I want to show you."

"Okay. Now I'm intrigued." Brinn held onto the side rail of the golf cart, studying the rough trail. The brush looked freshly cleared, but the ground was rough with roots and rocks. It was a pretty off-road trail for the golf cart. "Did you guys just cut this path?"

"Not exactly."

They rolled over a particularly bumpy patch, making Brinn's teeth rattle. "Ouch."

"That was the worst of it," Wanda promised. "This path has always been here, except in recent years it hadn't been maintained. When I said something about it, Cameron and Cam cleared it for me. It could use some grading, but with my beefed-up tires, the golf cart can handle it."

"But can your backside?" Brinn asked, rubbing at her achy hip. She wouldn't be surprised if she ended up with a bruise.

Wanda just chuckled. "You'll be fine. Trust me."

"This had better be good," Brinn said. Though she was already feeling better just being surrounded by the woods. The redwood-scented air soothed her. During the winter, she didn't get out nearly enough. She made a mental note to spend more time in nature. Witches always fared better when they filled their wells by spending time outdoors.

"Just wait for it." Wanda steered the cart around a giant redwood, and suddenly they were in a small clearing that overlooked a waterfall with a lagoon at the bottom. With the moon shining down, the entire area was bathed in silvery light.

Brinn let out a small gasp. "How is it possible I never knew this existed?"

"The previous owners had wards to keep people away." She gave Brinn a wicked little smile. "I got the impression they liked to go skyclad... often."

"That's not so unusual in a town of witches, I guess," Brinn said, trying to be diplomatic.

"Really?" Wanda laughed. "How many of us have ever stripped naked to perform rituals in the woods?"

"I dunno. Isn't that a thing the hardcore witches do?" Brinn held her hands out, palms up. "You know I'm mediocre at best."

Wanda *tsked*. "That's just because you don't care that much about magic or spells. You'd rather just read about witches and werewolves."

"True." Brinn had never really cared about being able to manipulate air. She'd never been great at it, so she mostly just stopped trying. And now it seemed others were trying to tell her that her real gift was communicating with the dead. No thank you.

Brinn's phone buzzed. It was a text from Austin.

Just checking to see what time you'll be home. I'm cooking.

Home. He'd called his place home. Brinn felt a pang of regret. How could she call that place home with Mathew Steele there? Brinn texted back. *Maybe I should stay away tonight. I could stay with Wanda.*

Why?

Brinn sucked in a breath. She didn't necessarily want to do this by text, but what choice did she have now? *Your dad? He doesn't seem thrilled to have me around.*

Don't worry about him. I tossed him out. He won't be back anytime soon.

What? Brinn blinked at the phone. *Why?*

He was out of line this morning. I won't have him talking to you like that, or telling me how to live my life. I'm making salmon with pesto. Will I see you?"

Brinn let out a sigh as she stared at the texts.

"Want to talk about it?" Wanda asked.

"No." But she handed Wanda the phone anyway.

"He threw his dad out for you?" Wanda said, sounding astonished. "Whoa. That's huge."

"His dad's an ass," Brinn said flatly.

"Sure. But if Austin threw him out because of the way he treated you... Well, that's commitment. That means he doesn't just care about you, he's putting you first. That's what partners do, Brinn. That's everything."

Brinn took in what her cousin said. Was that how Austin saw her? She knew he cared about her, but did he really see her as a partner? In her heart, she thought he did. But her head kept screaming at her to be cautious.

Wanda handed the phone back to her. "I can see you're overthinking this. Just text him back and tell him you'll be home in about an hour."

Brinn did as she was told. "There. It's done. But if things go south, don't be surprised to see me on your doorstep."

"They won't. Just trust your heart, Brinn. Turn those thoughts in your head off, and trust this. Trust him. I have a really good feeling about you guys this time."

Goddess, Brinn hoped her cousin was right. If Austin broke her heart again— She shook her head. Like Wanda said, it was time to trust her heart.

"Look." Wanda pointed at the lagoon below.

"What am I looking at?" Brinn squinted, trying to take in the surroundings.

"Over there on the far edge. There's a patch of white right at the tree line."

Brinn scanned the area. At first, she had no idea what her cousin was talking about, but then the patch of white moved toward the water's edge. Brinn let out a quiet gasp as she took in the pure white wolf, standing there looking sacred as if he were watching over the lagoon. "Oh my gosh. He's gorgeous."

"Isn't he?" Wanda smiled. "I first noticed him a month ago when I was out walking the property. He was just there, watching. It wasn't long after that when I stumbled on this path, and that's when I realized this is where he lives."

"Wow." Brinn turned wide eyes on her cousin. "You're really living a charmed life, aren't you?"

Wanda chuckled. "I don't know about that, but I am doing my best to appreciate the beauty of it all."

Tears stung Brinn's eyes. While she wasn't the jealous type, it was hard not to be envious of her cousin. Wanda had everything Brinn had ever wanted. A solid business, a home on a beautiful piece of land, a loving partner, and family. It wasn't all conventional, but it was special. Brinn had pieces of that. And maybe somehow she'd find a way to make it work with Austin. But if she kept being plagued by ghosts, how much of it would she enjoy?

Wanda sucked in an audible breath. "Brinn, look. Is that Zya down there?"

Brinn turned her attention back to the lagoon, spotted the wolf, and then followed the wolf's gaze to the woman walking toward the lagoon. "It certainly looks like it could be Zya. She has the same build." Brinn couldn't be sure. The woman was wearing a black cloak with a hood that hid most of her face. The woman paused just before she stepped into the water and then changed course, heading toward the wolf. "What is she doing? The wolf—" Brinn cut off her own words as she watched the woman hold her hand out for the wolf to sniff. When he was done, he turned his head into the palm of her hand, demanding pets. "Good Goddess. I guess this confirms that no matter how fierce they are, all it takes is a little ear scratch to win them over."

"It's incredible. She must be really special for a wolf to let her get that close," Wanda said.

Brinn nodded her agreement, completely in awe. "Have you seen Zya on your property before?"

Wanda shook her head. "No. But she might not even know it's ours. It's not that far from the national park with all the hiking trails."

That was true. Keating Hollow was in the valley just to the south of one of many national parks. And this area wasn't very developed, though now that the Pelshes had expanded their winery and Wanda and Cameron had built on the Copeland farm, progress was certainly being made. Still, Wanda wasn't the type to run anyone off as long as they were being respectful of the land.

"What is she doing?" Wanda asked, leaning forward and squinting into the moonlight.

Brinn focused on who she now knew for certain was Zya as she walked right into the lagoon. She'd lost the cloak, but was now in a loose white dress that she hadn't bothered to even hike up while wading into the water.

"Looks like some sort of spell or ritual. See the magic streaming off her fingertips?" Wanda pointed to the air above Zya's head.

The silver magic crackled in the air, hovering over Zya as if she were building up her stores, just waiting for the right time to unleash it. Suddenly Brinn felt her skin prickle and unease settled around her. She wrapped her arms around herself as if she were cold, trying to block out the sensation. But nothing worked. It just got worse and worse.

And then she saw why.

She sucked in a sharp breath and reached for Wanda's hand. "Do you see that?"

"The magic and the way the water is churning?" she asked.

"No. Oh gods. You don't see them." Brinn pressed a hand to her throat as she watched five ghosts appear from the woods and surround Zya. "There are ghosts, and they're circling her. We have to help." Brinn was out of the golf cart and running down the hill toward the lagoon before Wanda could respond.

One of the ghosts turned and stared Brinn in the eye. The old woman's face lit with glee as she started to float in Brinn's direction. As soon as she broke the circle, two of the other ghosts turned their attention toward Brinn and broke formation.

"That's right. Come at me," Brinn yelled, ready to be the decoy to help Zya. "I'm right here!"

"Brinn, no!" Zya yelled. The magic hovering above Zya suddenly burst outward, engulfing all five ghosts, wiping them out in one fell swoop.

Silence hung in the air. Brinn stared up at the inky sky and then at Zya, her heart racing. "How did you do that?"

Zya didn't say anything as she slogged out of the lagoon. The white wolf was waiting for her at the edge and fell into step with her as she walked toward Brinn.

"Wow," Wanda said from right behind Brinn.

Wow was right. Zya had just done the very thing Brinn had longed to do every time she'd been harassed by ghosts.

When Zya got within earshot, Wanda called, "That was impressive. Though I had no idea we had so many ghosts on the property."

"They're everywhere in Keating Hollow," Zya said. She glanced at the lagoon and then back at Wanda and Brinn. "Am I trespassing here?"

"Yes, but it's okay," Wanda said. "It belongs to me and Cam.

We haven't owned it all that long, so we're still getting the feel of things. The lagoon's magical, isn't it?"

Zya nodded. "I would've used the river, but I prefer a little privacy when I'm working my spells. If I'd known, I would've asked first."

"Don't worry about it at all," Wanda said.

"Where did the ghosts go?" Brinn asked.

Zya eyed her warily. "Away from me."

"Do you see them all the time?" Brinn pressed. "Do they talk to you and ask you to do things for them?"

"Yes, but," she glanced down at the wolf, "I have my ways of warding them off."

"Is it the wolf? Is he a protector? How did you do that in the lagoon? Is it a specific spell?" Brinn couldn't seem to stop herself from asking questions. "Will you show me? Do I need herbs or—"

Zya held a hand up, stopping her onslaught of questions. "I'm sorry, Brinn. I can't help you."

Brinn blinked and took a step back. "I'm sorry, what?"

Zya shook her head sadly. "I can't teach you. Not now. I'm sorry."

"Why?"

The shop owner took a step forward and placed a light hand on Brinn's shoulder. "I can't tell you my secrets. Not until your work is done."

"What work?" Brinn wanted to scream. She'd never been this close to having a solution to her problem. She couldn't let Zya walk away without any words of advice.

"You'll know when it's done." She dropped her hand to her side. "Come find me then."

"But—"

"Thank you, Wanda. I won't forget your kindness." She

touched the wolf's head briefly before the two of them walked back into the woods.

"That was… intense," Wanda said.

"Intense is one way to put it." A ghost had appeared the moment Zya stepped into the trees. She was a woman who looked to have passed in her early forties. She was pretty with blond hair, bright red lips, and wrinkles around her eyes when she smiled. The ghost held a cigarette and took a long puff, holding the smoke in for a few seconds before she blew it out.

Brinn closed her eyes and barely held in the scream that had bubbled up in her chest. "Go away," she said through her teeth.

"Nah. I don't think so. Not until you track down my old man. I need you to tell him something for me."

Brinn shook her head and slinked back to the golf cart.

"Sweet ride!" the ghost said as she got into the back seat. "Wish I'd have thrown down for one of these babies. It sure beats that broken down piece of shit my old man had me driving. The van was shaking all the time and had a belt that squealed like a pig. It's no wonder the brakes gave out and I ran into the world's largest cheese ball. I tell ya, of all the ways to go out, that's not the one I'd have chosen. I can still smell the mold that had formed at the bottom."

"Cheese ball?" Brinn asked.

Wanda frowned at her. "Are you calling me a cheese ball?"

"No." Brinn waved a hand at the back seat. "There's a ghost back there who claims she was killed by a cheese ball."

"What, did she choke on it?"

"Nope. She ran into it with her beater van," Brinn said. "And possibly had an allergic reaction to the mold."

"I'm allergic to penicillin," the ghost said. "But that's all water under the bridge. Right now, I need you to tell my old man that he needs to get to the doctor. Tell him to get that prostate looked at. If he doesn't, he's gonna be with me sooner than he expects."

Brinn turned to stare at the ghost. "That's it? You want me to warn him he needs to see a doctor? No evaluating his bedroom skills or trying to get me to cut his brake lines?"

"What? Hell, no. What kind of ghosts have you been hanging out with?" the spirit demanded.

"You really don't want to know," Brinn said, resting her head against the frame of the golf cart.

"It's really weird listening to you talk to ghosts when I can't hear their side of the conversation," Wanda said. "Weird but fascinating."

Brinn snorted. "I can imagine."

The ghost rattled off an address that was on the outskirts of Keating Hollow. "Tell Pickle to get that test, okay?"

"Pickle? That's his name?" Brinn asked.

"Yep. His real name is George. But if you call him Pickle, he'll know I sent you."

"Do I want to know the origin of that name?" Wanda asked with a laugh.

The ghost smirked. "Tell her it's exactly what she thinks." The ghost winked and then was gone.

"She's gone," Brinn said. "Remind me to find Pickle, aka George. This one's important."

"You got it." Wanda turned the golf cart around, turned on Fleetwood Mac, and danced in her seat as she took Brinn back to her car.

"Going old school, eh?" Brinn said, gesturing to the radio.

"After that lagoon scene, I just needed a little Stevie Nicks in my life," Wanda said.

"Yeah, I can see that," Brinn said, chuckling. After her

laughter faded away, she realized that might have been the first time she'd ever found the humor in her unwanted gift. Maybe seeing spirits wasn't always terrible. If only all the requests were so noble, maybe she could find a way to navigate her gift without losing her mind.

CHAPTER 22

$\mathcal{A}$ustin sat on his couch holding a cup of coffee with one hand and petting Dru with the other. He hadn't bothered to turn the living room lights on, so by the time the front door opened, he was sitting in the dark with just a sliver of light from the kitchen to keep him from sitting in total darkness.

He heard Brinn's footsteps, followed by Oz's nails on the hardwood. She paused just before she stepped out of the shadows to pick up Oz and give him kisses. Austin didn't blame her. The dog had been waiting at the door for her nearly since she'd left for work that morning.

"Hey," she said softly, walking into the dark living room with her arms full of dog.

"Hey yourself," he said, relieved to finally lay eyes on her. "I missed you."

She rewarded him with a small smile.

He hadn't known if he should say he missed her. If they were in a place where he could bare his heart to her. But he was past worrying about it. He wanted her. Now and for as long as she wanted him. After everything that had gone on with his father, he just wanted to lay his cards on the table. "I love you, Brinn."

She stood frozen in the middle of the room, clutching Oz, her eyes wide as she stared at him.

He gave her a half-smile. "Come on. You had to already know. I just needed to say it."

"I…" She shook her head as if changing her mind about what she wanted to say and walked over to the couch. After placing Oz next to Dru, she crouched in front of him. With one hand on his knee and the other cupping his face, she said, "I've always loved you, Austin. Even when I hated you for leaving. It was always you. It's always going to be you."

He searched her blue eyes, looking for what, he wasn't sure. Truth? Trust? Permanence? He hoped she saw all three and more in his gaze. "I'm sorry for what my father said about you this morning. He has no idea what he's talking about."

She leaned in and gave him a soft kiss on his lips before pulling back. "I know. I just don't want to be in the middle of anything."

"You're not," he insisted. "I told him to leave, and when he wouldn't, I called Drew to remove him."

"You did what?" she asked, sounding as if she didn't believe him.

"He refused to leave, and I refused to let him stay here. We were at an impasse, so I did what I had to do. He left before the deputy sheriff became involved."

"I really don't want to be the one standing between you and your father," Brinn said.

Austin took her hand and gently guided her until she was

sitting in his lap. "The only person coming between me and my father is my father. Brinn, he already interfered once before. I won't let him do it again. I love you. If he can't be civil to the woman I want to spend the rest of my life with, then he's not welcome in my house."

Brinn's breath caught, and tears welled in her bright blue eyes. A single tear spilled down her cheek, and he brushed it away with his thumb.

"Are those happy tears, or did I upset you?" he asked, praying it was the former.

She let out a small huff of laughter. "More like overwhelmed tears." Brinn snuggled into him. With her head on his shoulder, she said, "This is the first time all day that I've felt warm and safe."

Austin wrapped his arms around her and pressed a kiss to her temple. "I want to help you feel warm and safe for the rest of our lives."

She pulled away and looked him in the eye. With her lips twitching, she said, "If that's a proposal, I'm afraid you're going to have to do better. And I want a ring."

He chuckled. "Fair enough. I'll consider a flash mob. How's that?"

"Don't you dare!" She swatted at his chest. "You know how much I hate being the center of attention in front of an audience. All I'm asking for is a real proposal and maybe a little romance."

"This is romantic." He caressed her jaw with one hand. "Just you me and the pups. The cats are upstairs, but I can get them if it makes you feel better."

"You're right, it is romantic." She put her hand over his heart. "Ask me properly when we both haven't had the worst days, and I promise I'll say yes." Brinn leaned in and brushed her lips over his, making his heart ache for her.

Without another word, he tightened his grip on her and stood. "I'm no longer that interested in dinner. You?"

She shook her head.

"Good." Before he carried her upstairs, he said, "Get Dru. She'll never make it upstairs on that bum leg."

Brinn reached down and scooped up the puppy.

"Perfect. Now let's go to bed." He ignored the kitchen light and carried Brinn and Dru upstairs while Oz followed. After he gently placed Brinn on the bed, he carried Dru over to her crate, and just as Austin knew he would, Oz climbed in with her. He said goodnight to them both and returned to Brinn.

She sat up on the edge of the bed, grabbed his shirt, and pulled him in so he was standing between her legs. With her hands running up over his chest she said, "I heard everything you said earlier. Now all I want is for you to show me."

"Gladly." With his heart full, Austin gently pushed her back onto the bed and did his best to worship every inch of her.

AUSTIN WAS busy placing waffles on a platter when the doorbell rang.

Brinn, who'd been frying the bacon, turned off the pan and said, "I'll get it."

He watched her glide out of the kitchen, a relaxed smile on her face, and felt a tug of pride. He'd been the one to put that look on her face, and given half a chance, he'd do it again and again and again.

"Austin?" Brinn called. "I think you'd better come here."

Dammit. That didn't sound good. Austin turned the waffle

maker off and hurried into the foyer where Brinn was staring at an unfamiliar man on the front porch.

"Austin Steele?" he asked.

"Yes."

"You've been served." A manilla envelope appeared out of nowhere and was thrust at Austin. He took it, already knowing what it would be. Scowling, Austin closed the door and strode back into the kitchen. Oz popped up from his dog bed and started to growl.

"You're a little late, buddy," Brinn said, leaning down to scratch his ear. "I'm sure your dad appreciates the support, though."

Austin snorted. "Yeah. I do. Can you send Buffy after him, though? Those claws of hers could really do some damage if she tried."

Brinn smiled at him. "I would if she wasn't sleeping in the sun on the back of your couch right now. And before you ask, Willow and Xander are sharpening their claws on the cat tree in your office."

"There's a cat tree in my office?" he asked, wondering when that arrived.

She shrugged. "I noticed Willow trying to use your chair and grabbed it last night on my way home. I brought it in this morning while you were still getting your beauty rest."

He placed the waffles and bacon on the table. "Someone wore me out."

Brinn walked over to him, wrapped her arms around his waist, and took her time kissing him.

Austin wasn't complaining. If he had his way, he'd take her right back upstairs and spend the day worshipping her. However, he knew he wouldn't be able to stop thinking about that manilla envelope. He needed to open it and notify his lawyer at the very least.

"Okay," Brinn said breathlessly. "As much as I wouldn't mind doing more of that, the bacon is calling my name." She disengaged from him and took a seat at the table.

"I see where I am in the hierarchy. Bacon first, then waffles, and maybe me?"

"Bacon, coffee, waffles, and then you. But don't be upset. I didn't eat anything but sugar yesterday. The bacon is some much-needed protein."

"I've got some pro—"

"Don't say it," she said through a laugh.

He couldn't help it. She was too infectious. He laughed too. This was just one of the many things he'd missed about her. Brinn was a hard worker, always true to her word, and would do anything for the people she cared about. But her sense of humor was just as fierce as her work ethic and loyalty. "Okay. Eat. I'll figure out what fresh hell this legal document brings us."

Brinn scowled at the packet of papers he pulled out of the envelope.

"I share your sentiment," he said and got to work reading, while Brinn nearly devoured her meal. The longer he read the letter from his father's lawyer, the angrier he became. Finally he threw the papers down and got up to retrieve his phone.

"What is it, Austin?" Brinn asked, putting her fork down to give him her full attention.

"He's claiming Gran wasn't of sound mind when she changed her trust. The bastard is trying to say she was suffering from an undiagnosed form of dementia."

"He can't do that," Brinn said as all the hairs on her arm

stood up. "How could he even make that claim without access to her medical records?"

"Trust me. If there's anything of interest, he'll find a way." Austin shook his head. "He always does."

"There's not, is there?" Brinn asked, worry in her gaze.

"Not that I know of." Austin paced the room and then retreated to his office to make a call to his lawyer. A couple of minutes later, he returned to find Brinn cleaning up the kitchen. "You don't have to do this. Come on. Let's finish eating. I'll fill you in on the plan."

Brinn kissed him on the cheek and joined him at the table. "Okay." She rubbed her hands together and in a conspiratorial tone said, "What's the plan? I'm in. Need a ghost to haunt him? I'm pretty sure I could make that happen."

He chuckled. Damn, she was cute. "We'll make that our backup plan. For now, the lawyer is going to get in touch with her doctor and find out if there is anything legally to this lawsuit. We don't know if we'll get any information unless compelled by the court, but I think they might give it to me. She'd given the doctor permission to talk to me before. In the meantime, she wants me to get written statements from her friends, indicating they didn't see any issues with her judgment."

"Isn't that something the lawyer would normally do?" Brinn asked as she picked up a piece of bacon.

"I said I'd do it. Lorna, the attorney, has court today. She said the sooner we respond the sooner we can get this thrown out." Austin knew there was no real hurry to settle this case. Neither he nor Gideon were in a rush to get the art and music program underway, but the very idea that his father was doing this ate Austin up inside. The sooner this was over, the sooner he could get his dad out of his life.

"Okay. What do you need me to do?" Brinn asked. "I have today off."

"Come to lunch with me and Caroline?" he asked.

She stared down at her half-eaten waffles and laughed. "Sure. Looks like I'm gonna need a workout later."

He closed his hand over hers. "Don't worry about that. I already have plans."

CHAPTER 23

*B*rinn followed Austin into Woodlines, the restaurant Caroline had picked for lunch.

"There she is," Austin said, nodding toward a table near the back that was tucked away for a bit of privacy.

"Who's that with her?" Brinn asked. Caroline was facing them, but another woman seated next to her with short gray hair was bobbing her head as she talked animatedly.

"Ms. Betty."

Brinn raised her eyebrows. "Really? I didn't know she was coming."

"Caroline already had plans with her today. And since I already promised Ms. Betty a lunch, I said it was fine."

Brinn clutched his arm. "You do know the entire town will know about this lawsuit by this afternoon if you include her in the conversation, right?"

He turned to her, his eyes lit with fire. But when he spoke, his lips curved up into an evil smile. "Do you know what kind of damage Ms. Betty could do to a case like this? She loved Gran. Whether it's true or not, she'll have the entire town believing that Gran could've written a Pulitzer prize winning paper in the days before she passed. Public sentiment will not be on my dad's side. And as soon as they hear about the arts and music program, well... You can see where I'm going with this."

"Well played, Mr. Steele," she said. "Well played."

He leaned down to kiss her cheek, and they were suddenly serenaded with catcalls and wolf whistles by the two women who were waiting for them. Austin's face turned a mild shade of pink as he turned to the older women. "Good afternoon. It looks like someone started in on the cocktails early."

Ms. Betty raised her pink drink and nodded enthusiastically. "There's no time like the present to enjoy oneself. Wouldn't you say, Austin?"

"I would." He pulled out a chair for Brinn and then took the seat next to her. "And honestly, a little booze probably isn't bad considering the topic of conversation."

"What is it, dear?" Caroline asked, placing a soft hand over his.

He took a deep breath and explained the lawsuit against the trust. "Lorna says it's frivolous and likely won't go anywhere, but she asked me to get letters from you both describing Gran's mental state as you knew it in the weeks up to her passing."

"How dare he?" Ms. Betty said, slamming her drink down on the table. "Smearing Peggy's name like that? Why, I'll put fire ants in his drawers. The ungrateful, money-grubbing fart head."

Brinn sputtered with laughter. *Fart head?* she mouthed to Austin.

"Ms. Betty, you have quite the way with words," he said diplomatically. "But let's forgo the fire ants for now."

"Fine. We'll revisit that later. But I will most definitely write that letter. I can get half a dozen of my friends at the retirement village to write one, too. How dare your father do this, and after everything she did for him, too? Bailing him out like that, setting him back up after his treatments."

Brinn watched as realization washed over Austin's features. That clearly was information he hadn't known previously.

"That's why she only left him a small portion of her estate," he said quietly as if talking to himself.

"Yes," Caroline said. "She told him she'd help him once and after that he was on his own."

Austin glanced at his grandmother's best friend. "I know I asked you before, but I have to ask again. Do you know why she left almost half of her estate to Gideon Alexander?"

"I really don't. But we both know she wouldn't have done it lightly. And while I agree it's strange that she didn't leave an explanation, I know she had a good reason."

Everyone was quiet for a while until Ms. Betty slammed her hand on the table. "You know what Mathew needs?"

A slap to the head? Brinn thought to herself. *Lessons in humility and compassion and honor?* There was a lot Brinn thought Mathew Steele was lacking.

"A good roll in the hay. I'd offer, because that thing is just up my alley. If I wasn't so mad, I'd screw the—"

Austin coughed and held his hand up. "I think we get the picture. Thank you. If you think there's someone who can, um… help him work out his aggressions, maybe point them his way."

Ms. Betty threw her head back and cackled. "I knew having lunch with you would be fun. We'll have to do this again, Austin Steele."

Brinn couldn't help smiling at them. The day had started out stressful, but leave it to Ms. Betty to defuse the tension.

THE DAYS after learning about the lawsuit proved to turn more and more stressful. Not only was Brinn continually plagued by ghosts when she was away from Austin's house, but Austin was also getting increasingly agitated. While a judge had deemed the lawsuit frivolous, that hadn't stopped his father's attorney from going forward in the form of appeals.

There was discovery that required Austin to comb through all of his grandmother's files and depositions. Plus all the lawyer fees. Austin insisted he had the funds to cover it, but that didn't mean he wasn't resentful. And in the middle of all of that, he'd had to fly back and forth to Los Angeles to keep his business afloat. He had a studio manager, but there were some clients who only wanted to work with him. He was distracted and frustrated to the point that Brinn was starting to worry about him.

"I just don't know if it's worth all this hassle," Brinn told Miranda one day while they were both at Incantation Café. "Austin isn't himself. His relationship with his father has always been strained, but now it's downright hostile. I know the art and music program is worth fighting for; I just don't know if it's worth Austin's mental health."

"We both know it isn't, but do you really think Austin is going to drop this? I think it's the principle of the thing at this point, don't you?" Miranda asked. "Plus, from what I gather, Austin's father has used money and threats against those he loves for far too long. I think his mental health will take an even bigger hit if he doesn't fight him. He needs this win. It's not about the money so much as it is what's right and wrong and how much Austin's willing to let his father take from him."

Brinn sat with her words, knowing there was truth there. "You're right. But I just can't sit around and watch him suffer like this."

"You could do something about it," a raspy voice said into her ear.

Brinn waved the ghost away like she was a pesky fly. It was just a given now that when she went out a spirit would find her. She'd learned that if she ignored them, they went away faster.

"That's not going to work on me," the spirit said.

Brinn groaned and pressed her face into her hands. "Make it stop."

"I would if I could," Miranda said sympathetically. "You know, after all these years of writing about the paranormal, you'd think I'd know some tricks to make ghosts go away."

"That would be nice. Though Zya does, but she won't share them with me. She says I have work to do. But I already warned that guy about his prostate. And I helped a spirit help her daughter find a locket. Not to mention the one where I stopped that sixty-seven-year-old woman from sleeping with the man who has a couple of STIs. That was crossing the line into what I should and shouldn't be expected to do, don't you think?"

Miranda's lips twitched with amusement, but she managed to keep herself from laughing. "You're providing a public service. You should feel good about that."

"All I feel is annoyed," Brinn groused. "How long am I going to have to keep this up before I can get some peace?"

The spirit hovering behind Brinn said, "I have something you can do."

Brinn scowled but still turned to look at her. Until she knew what job she was supposed to do, she wasn't exactly in a position to ignore anything that seemed worthy. "What's that?"

"You can go talk to Mathew Steele yourself. He's the one you need to help."

"What?" Brinn asked, blinking at the spirit. "How?"

"You'll see." The ghost finger-waved and then floated out of the café right through the window.

"What was that about?" Miranda asked.

"The ghost told me to go help Mathew Steele." There was a pit in Brinn's stomach. Surely the ghost was wrong? How could Brinn possibly help him? And why would she want to? His aim was to take Peggy Steele's money and to screw his son and Gideon out of creating a worthy arts and music program.

"Help him do what?"

Brinn threw her hands up in the air. "I have no idea, but there's no way I'm visiting Mathew Steele. That's just a recipe for disaster."

"It definitely seems like it." Miranda stood and tugged on her coat. "I have to go by the bookstore. I promised Yvette I'd sign some more books that were due in yesterday. Want to walk with me?"

"Sure." Brinn followed the author out of the café and down the street to the bookstore. The moment they stepped inside, Brinn knew something was wrong. The shelves needed to be stocked, and Yvette was on the phone, pacing the store, her face set into a scowl.

Miranda walked over to the section where her books were usually stocked, frowned, and retreated back to where Brinn was waiting for Yvette to get off the phone. "Do you know why the shelves are so empty?"

Brinn shook her head. "We had a few delayed shipments,

but they were supposed to be in last night. Yvette and Jacob were going to stock this morning." Brinn strode through the store to check the storage room. It was empty. There wasn't even any cardboard waiting to be broken down and recycled. An ache formed in her stomach. This was unprecedented. They sometimes had stocking issues, but not with every book from every publisher including indies. Something was very wrong.

Brinn hurried back up to the counter and overheard Yvette telling the person she was speaking to that there had been a mistake. She wasn't behind on any bills. Her credit card was even paid in full. There was no reason why they should be denied shipments. When she hung up, she tossed the phone onto the counter and hung her head in frustration.

"I can't believe this," Yvette said.

"What's going on?" Brinn moved to stand next to her.

"Our account has a hold on it. The distributor won't send us any books because supposedly we are in breach of our contract, whatever that means." Yvette stared at the ceiling. "All these shipping delays were really because our account has this hold on it. Not because there's a backup at the printers or distributor. It's our account, and I can't get anyone on the phone who can tell me why."

"This is highly unusual, isn't it? I've never heard of something like this before." Brinn walked behind the counter and tapped on the computer screen.

"This only happens when a bookstore stops paying their bills. That's not the case here. I haven't paid anything because we haven't gotten a shipment in two weeks."

"Let me look at the account and see if there's anything unusual," Brinn said, fearing she'd done something wrong when placing an order. She'd taken over the ordering for

Yvette not long after they adopted their second child so that Yvette could work less.

When Brinn went to log in, the site kicked her out, indicating that her password had been changed. She glanced up at Yvette. "Did you change the password on our account?"

Yvette shook her head.

Brinn scowled. "We've been hacked."

"I told you to go see Mathew Steele," the raspy-voiced ghost said into her ear.

Brinn stiffened and turned to stare at the ghost who'd just appeared. "Are you saying he had something to do with this?"

"Doesn't it seem obvious?" She pumped her eyebrows and then faded away.

"I think I know what's happened," Brinn said through clenched teeth. "I have to go."

"Wait," Yvette called. "What's going on?"

"Mathew Steele is messing with your business because of me. I'm not letting him get away with it. Not this time." She swept out of the store, her entire body vibrating with rage. Mathew Steele's time of messing with the people she loved was about to come to an end.

CHAPTER 24

*B*rinn stormed into the house and headed straight for the office where she knew she'd find Austin. But when she got there, the office was empty. "Dammit," she muttered.

How was she going to confront Mathew Steele if she had no idea where he was staying?

After rummaging through the papers on the desk, she finally found some legal paperwork that had his address. "There! Got him."

She grabbed her keys, paused to love on the animals for a minute, and then took off again. Just as she was unlocking her car, a horn blew, catching her attention.

Wanda was in her SUV, her head hanging out the window. "Where are you headed?"

"To confront Austin's father." She tried to yank her door open but fumbled when she realized it was still locked.

"Get in," Wanda said. "I'll drive."

Brinn raised an eyebrow. "Why are you here?"

"Yvette called me. She didn't want you dealing with Austin's dad on your own. It's probably better to have a witness anyway." She gave her cousin a quick smile. "Besides, I'm your ride or die. Who else would go?"

Ride or die. Brinn wouldn't have thought to classify their relationship in such a way. She'd always thought Abby was Wanda's person, or maybe it was Cameron now. But Brinn? They were just cousins.

"Why are you looking at me like that? I have your back, okay? Now get in." She pushed the passenger side door open. "Let's kick some dad butt."

Brinn couldn't help the smile that claimed her lips, and she did as she was told. Once she was belted in and Wanda was headed down the street, she said, "Ride or die? Since when?"

Wanda glanced at her, surprise on her face. "Since always. What makes you think otherwise?"

Brinn shrugged. "I dunno. I just... You were always closer to Abby."

"I can have more than one ride or die, Brinn. You, Abby, Cameron, Blake." She turned onto the main road that led into Keating Hollow. "I'm sorry if I made you feel otherwise."

Shaking her head, Brinn reached over and squeezed Wanda's hand. "It's probably just me. After Austin left, I had a hard time feeling close to people again."

Wanda squeezed her hand back. "We've done a lot of growing up over the last few years, haven't we?"

"We have."

"Just remember I'm here for you," Wanda said. "And I'll cut someone if they hurt you, so Mathew Steele better watch out."

Brinn smiled at her, but then sobered. Whatever Mathew Steele was up to, it would stop now. She was done putting up with his bullying.

"Where am I headed?" Wanda asked.

Brinn rattled off an address. Wanda nodded and sped up.

Mathew's place was a few miles out of town off a dirt road, surrounded by a thicket of trees. When the big blue Victorian house came into view, Brinn leaned forward, her eyes wide at the scene in front of her.

Austin was standing in the front yard, yelling at his dad, who was just standing there on the wide porch with his arms folded over his chest.

"Did you know Austin was here?" Wanda asked.

"I had no idea." As soon as Wanda stopped the car, Brinn jumped out and ran over to where Austin was belting out a string of insults. She wondered if he'd already figured out that his dad was interfering in her life again. But as he continued to yell at Mathew, Brinn gathered his diatribe had everything to do with the lawsuit and not the bookstore.

"If you think this is going to repair anything between us, you've lost your ever-loving mind!" Austin shouted. "If anything, this will put a rift between us so large that you'll never see your grandchildren," Austin warned.

Mathew's gaze landed on Brinn, his eyes going cold. "You are not welcome here."

"I'm sure that's true," Brinn shot back. "But you lost your right to be left alone when you messed with Yvette's business. I see you're still using any means possible to try to keep Austin away from me. The only question is, why? Why do you care so much that we're together?"

"He messed with Yvette's store?" Austin asked.

Brinn slipped her hand into his. "Yes. He somehow got her distributer to suspend her account. Now she can't get books. No books. No store. No store, no job for me."

"You don't know what you're talking about," Mathew said with a sneer.

"Is that true?" Austin asked his father, but judging by the murderous look on his face he was already convinced of his father's guilt.

Mathew stepped off his porch, moving toward Austin. "Look, son. We need to stop this feuding. All I'm doing is looking out for you. That's all I've ever done."

"You're looking out for *you!*" Wanda yelled at Mathew. "How dare you come to this town and treat my cousin like she's somehow beneath you. Or use her to get your way with your son. You're a pathetic man who doesn't deserve Austin."

"Leave," Mathew said to Wanda and then turned his attention to Austin. "Or I'll call the authorities and have her removed." He nodded toward Brinn. "Her, too. This conversation is between me and you."

"Brinn and Wanda aren't going anywhere," Austin said. "If you want to call the authorities, we'll have them investigate the situation over at Hollow Books."

Mathew pulled out his phone and started tapping at the screen.

"I can't believe he's actually calling them," Brinn said.

"I can," the raspy-voiced ghost said. She'd suddenly appeared right beside Brinn.

Another ghost appeared. This time it was the tall woman with the long black dress. "He's always been the bully." She glanced at the other ghost. "Nice to see you again, Cass."

"You, too, Shondra," Cass said with a nod.

They both turned to Brinn.

"It's time," Cass said, her raspy voice full of conviction.

"Time for what?" Brinn asked.

"To use that gift of yours," Shondra said, eyeing Mathew. "This will never end until you do."

"I don't understand," Brinn said. "What won't end?"

"Get off my property!" Mathew bellowed as he lurched forward, trying to grab Brinn.

Austin moved so fast that Brinn barely had time to process what was happening before Austin decked his father. Mathew Steele landed flat on his back, sputtering blood from a split lip.

"Holy shit!" Cass said, her expression full of glee. "If you knew how many times I've wanted to do that." She threw her head back and cackled. "It couldn't have happened to a better person."

"You knew Mathew Steele?" Brinn asked her.

"Not exactly, but we are connected to him," Cass said. "That's why we're here. To help you."

"Help me do what?" Brinn asked again. "I don't understand what you want me to do."

"We want you to use your gift. It's the only way forward," Shondra said. "For everyone. You, Austin, Mathew." She glanced at Cass. "Us. All you need to do is open yourself to your gift. Call the spirits to you. Then you'll see."

Fear crawled up Brinn's spine. She'd spent years trying to live ghost free, staying in Keating Hollow so that she'd be free from being followed or harassed. All she'd ever wanted was peace. And now these ghosts were telling her the only way the nightmare unfolding in front of her would end was if she embraced the very thing she'd never wanted.

Mathew was back on his feet, his fists flying as he threw punches at his son. Austin was too quick for him though, and quickly got him in a headlock. Austin wasn't a violent man. Brinn hadn't ever witnessed him lay hands on anyone before. This fight with his father was a culmination of everything that had happened, not just over the last few weeks, but since his dad had tried to control him years ago when he'd threatened

Brinn's grandmother's business. If there was a way that Brinn could end this for him, she'd do it.

She turned back to the two ghosts. "You're saying if I open myself to the spirits it's somehow going to fix this?"

"It should," Shondra said, her gaze fixated on Mathew. "It will end his aggression."

That was enough for Brinn. If Mathew called a ceasefire, Austin would too. In fact, Austin was already trying to defuse the situation. He *had* thrown the first punch, but since then, all he'd tried to do was stay out of the way of his father's fists.

Mathew shifted and somehow got the best of Austin. He flipped his son over his shoulder, sending Austin to the ground. He landed with a thud so hard it had to have knocked the wind out of him. Austin came up, fists flying, and Brinn suddenly had the awful thought that if someone didn't do something, they were going to kill each other.

"Tell me what to do," she demanded of the two ghosts that were staring at her.

"Do what?" Wanda asked.

Brinn shook her head at her. "Not now, Wanda. Whatever happens next, just pray that it's the right thing."

"You need to invite the spirits into your space," Shondra said. "Call them to you. You'll be like a magnet. They won't be able to stop themselves."

"And what happens after that?" Brinn asked in a trembling voice.

"You set them free," Cass said, her voice full of kindness. "They're only here because they have to be. You have the power to end their... *our* suffering."

Brinn took a moment to really look at the two ghosts who were standing in front of her. "If I'm successful, you'll get to move on?"

"That's the hope," Shondra said with a nod. "We won't be the only ones either."

Brinn sucked in a deep breath. That would be a lot more satisfying than tracking down left-behind loved ones just to tell them the mailbox key had fallen into a boot. She nodded to Shondra. "Okay, I'm ready."

Shondra moved to stand next to Cass. The pair of ghosts huddled together a few feet from where the fighting was still in progress. They both looked excited, but their excitement was tempered with a fair amount of fear. Brinn supposed if she was a ghost and was on the verge of being sent to her final haunting place, she'd be a little anxious, too.

"How do I do this?" Brinn asked the two ghosts.

They both shrugged and then took another step back.

Brinn guessed her crash course in embracing her gift was over. It was time to just try something. Anything.

She pictured what Zya had looked like when she was in the lagoon and mimicked her movements. Although Zya had ultimately repelled the spirits, she'd first called them to her. And that was what Brinn intended to do. Raising her arms, she tilted her head back and called, "Spirits, hear my call! I'm here, ready and waiting to help you free yourselves."

Immediately, two ghosts popped into existence. Two very familiar ghosts.

"Gran!" she cried, desperately wanting to hug her. The other was Peggy Steele, Austin's grandmother. They both walked over to Brinn.

"Good for you, baby," her grandmother said. "Call the spirits. Make them hear you."

Brinn cut her gaze to Peggy. Austin's grandmother was staring down at her son and grandson in disgust. "Mathew Steele," she barked.

Mathew froze, his fist still in the air as he glanced around.

"Can he see you?" Brinn asked.

She shook her head. "Not yet. But he will. And then the shit is going to hit the fan. Keep going, dear. Let's see this through to the end."

Brinn raised her hands again, but this time she closed her eyes and spoke directly to the Goddess. "Send me the spirits who are trapped. Let me free them from the ties that bind them. I'm open. Waiting. Ready to serve."

The wind picked up, whipping Brinn's hair around her face. Thunder rippled all around them, and in the next moment, a bolt of lightning flickered through the sky.

"That's it," her grandmother said. "It's working. They're coming."

Brinn didn't dare open her eyes. She was too afraid it would stop her from doing what she knew deep in her soul that she needed to do. "I'm your vessel. Come to me. Free your souls from this earth."

A blood-curdling scream pierced the air, followed by a roar of outrage. Brinn kept her arms up, her mind open, and waited as the world raged around her.

"She's impressive, isn't she?" Brinn's grandmother asked someone. "I couldn't be prouder if I tried."

Brinn reached higher, as if trying to reach for the sky itself. Pride filled her soul, knowing her grandmother approved. That she was worthy of that pride. "Come to me!" Brinn called one last time.

"That's it," Shondra said. "It's almost over, Cass."

Brinn's eyes popped open and she spotted the two ghosts clutching each other, both with a look of shock and awe on their faces.

"What is?" Brinn asked, but when she followed their gazes,

her mouth fell open and she suddenly understood what all of this was about.

Austin had taken a dozen steps back from his father and was staring in horror as a ghost was being ripped from his body. The ghost was doing everything in its power to hang on, and even started to merge with Mathew Steele again. But Brinn instinctively knew it was because she'd let up on her own magic.

She immediately raised her arms, pointing in the ghost's direction. "Spirits of Keating Hollow, come to me. I call to you to set you free. To rid you of these human bonds. Come to me!"

The ghost twisted and writhed, trying to completely merge with Mathew, but he had little success. And when Brinn stepped closer, the ghost's expression turned panicked.

"Release Mathew Steele!" Brinn ordered. "Your time here is done."

The air picked up, the wind blowing harder than it had in months. And suddenly, the tall ghost of a man released Mathew Steele. Austin's father fell to the ground, his face chalk-white and his fingers shaking from the exertion.

"You!" the tall ghost shouted as he pointed at her. "You're responsible for this. I knew you were trouble. If only I'd have gotten rid of you sooner. If Mathew Steele had any spine at all, he'd have killed you when he had a chance."

Wanda let out a gasp and stalked forward. "If you speak to her that way again, you'll die for a second time."

"You can see him?" Brinn asked, shaken by what the ghost had said.

"Yeah." She scowled at the ghost still hovering near them. "Keep away from her, or I'll find a way to send you somewhere truly awful, like West Texas."

Brinn suppressed a snort, loving that Wanda was there defending her as if there was something she could do to harm the ghost.

Austin appeared at her side, his arm wrapped around her waist. "You're not welcome here," he said through clenched teeth as he stared at the too thin ghost. "You were never welcome here."

"You can see him, too?" Brinn asked, her voice a little shaky.

"Yes. I can also see both of our grandmothers, the two ghosts standing off to the side there, and about a dozen more that have formed a circle around us." He tightened his grip on her. "Are you all right?"

She peered at his red face, noting a cut above his eyes from the fighting. "Are you?"

"I'll live."

"Me, too," she said.

"You," Mathew said, staring at the ghost. "You're the man who died that night after that awful car crash."

"Who else would I be?" The ghost scowled at him. "You took my life, so I took yours. I'd still have it if it weren't for that ghost magnet over there." He pointed at Brinn. "I told you to get rid of her."

Mathew glanced at Brinn and then at Austin. He closed his eyes and shook his head. "My son loves her."

The ghost grunted in disappointment.

Shondra and Cass moved forward, standing right in front of him. Cass reached up and slapped him across the face. "You're the reason I've been stuck here for so long, you selfish bastard. All because you couldn't face moving on to the next realm. Well, I'm done. You got that? I'm out of here."

"I wasn't stopping you before," the ghost shot back.

"Oh no?" She held up her ring finger, showing off a small

diamond ring. "This is what kept me here. That wedding you talked me into kept me here. Our binding. Now I'm calling the shots. You're not invading some poor man's body again, not over a senseless accident. Especially one that happened on a dark rainy night when no one was really at fault." She glanced at Shondra. "She's ready to move on, too."

Shondra looked pained as she watched them.

"Shonny?" the ghost said. "You stayed for me?"

"I stayed because I had to," she said, her voice flat. "But if I'd had a choice, I'd have moved on right away. Who wants to stick around for a decade, attached to her lover's wife? You son of a bitch." She held her hand up, showing off an even bigger ring. "You asked me to marry you when you were already spoken for. The moment I said yes, I was bound to you. And look what you gave me. Years of roaming this earth, dead, with your wife while you invaded some man's body and made him do horrible things to his family, just so you wouldn't get ejected. Pathetic."

"I—"

"No one wants to hear it, John. No one," Cass said, cutting him off. "It's time to go." She held her hand out to Shondra. The two women ghosts held hands and walked away from John toward a faint white light that was just to the right of the house. Together, they stepped into the light, and when they disappeared, so did John. His body started to fade, but before he disappeared completely, the wind picked him up and sent him straight into the light.

The ghosts that had encircled them followed, one by one, walking into the light until the only ghosts left were Violet Taylor and Peggy Steele.

Brinn turned to her grandmother. "This is what everyone meant when they said I needed to embrace my gift, right?"

She gave Brinn a soft smile. "Yes, baby. Now that you know how to help them, you can control it better."

"My gift is to help them cross over?" she asked, finally putting it all together.

Her grandmother nodded. "For a long time, I thought your gift was like mine. I could just talk to them, ward them off, help others communicate if it was important enough. It's why I set wards up here in Keating Hollow. To keep you shielded from it as long as possible. But after I passed on, I realized it was different. Your light is magical. Every ghost who sees you knows you're calling them home. Some will embrace it. Some will flee. But they know you're special. That's why you get so many talking to you."

"If you set wards up to keep me insulated, why am I suddenly seeing ghosts everywhere?" Brinn asked.

"My spells are only good for so long, love. Besides, it was time for you to know." She nodded at Austin. "You're the only one who could help him finally know what happened to his father."

Brinn stared at Austin, who was busy helping his father up to the house. Mathew Steele was clutching his son's arm and moving like a broken man, his head down.

"Once all the secrets come out, the healing can begin," her gran said.

"I hope so," Brinn said with a wary sigh.

"Go on. Peggy will help put all the pieces together." Her gran nodded toward the house.

"I'm not sure I should. Austin's dad made it perfectly clear how he feels about me."

"That was the ghost John talking," she reassured her granddaughter. "Go on now. It's time for me to make my own journey into the light."

Brinn's eyes instantly filled with tears as she shook her head. "No, Gran. Not right now. I feel like I just got you back."

"Oh, sweetie, I'm always with you. Right here." She pointed to Brinn's heart. "My job here is done. It's time for me to find my resting spot. But I'll always be with you, Brinn. You know that, right?"

Brinn nodded even as tears streamed down her face.

"It's not a goodbye, Brinn," her grandmother insisted. "We'll be reunited one day when it's your turn to cross over into the light. And when you do, I'll be waiting on the other side with open arms."

Brinn threw her arms around her grandmother and was surprised when she was met with solid flesh. She'd been expecting something a little more ethereal. But she wasn't complaining. If this was the last hug she was getting from her gran, she was going to make it count. Brinn closed her eyes, held on tight, and whispered, "I love you."

"I love you, too, baby girl." The words were barely a whisper as her grandmother slipped from her arms and without looking back, walked into the light.

The tears streamed uncontrollably down Brinn's cheeks. The pain in her chest was almost too much to bear.

"Come on, Brinn," Wanda said softly, steering her toward the house. "Let's get you inside before any more ghosts come calling."

Brinn blinked at her. She'd completely forgotten that her cousin had been there, watching it all go down. "Did you see her, Wanda? My gran?"

"I did. She looked wonderful, as always," Wanda said. "Though I question her taste in hair dye."

A laugh bubbled up and burst from Brinn's lips. "She always was partial to that bleach blond color."

"I guess it suits her," Wanda said. "I sure hope my gran is watching over me the way yours did. That's pretty awesome. You know that, right?"

Brinn nodded. "Yes. It is. But now that she's gone, I'm really going to miss her."

"I know." Wanda tucked her arm through Brinn's and led her toward the house. "I think it's time for some more answers, don't you?"

"Yes. I'm more than ready."

CHAPTER 25

*A*ustin paced his father's rental house, still unsure of where to start. It had been quite the shock to see that ghost literally ripped from the man. And while a lot of questions had been answered, there were still some significant ones that needed to be addressed.

Especially the part about his dad sabotaging Brinn's place of work. Oh, he'd heard what the ghost had said. He just needed to hear it from his dad.

"I'm sorry, son," Mathew Steele said from his place on the shabby couch. "I never meant to hurt you. I never meant to hurt anyone."

"Not even Brinn?" he asked, ice still in his tone.

His father shook his head. "All of that was John. I swear it. He bribed one of my contacts at the distributor to get them to disrupt the orders from Hollow Books."

"And you didn't do anything about it?" Austin accused.

"Austin," Peggy Steele said, "John was too strong. Your father couldn't fight him off."

"Are you sure about that? What about this lawsuit? Was that John, too?"

Mathew nodded. "It was. He wanted the money for himself."

Austin narrowed his eyes at his father. He desperately wanted to believe that the father he'd known over the past decade had been a product of that other spirit taking over his body, but that seemed awfully convenient. "Are you saying you had no free will at all, and everything you've done, the drinking, the threats, the lawsuit, was all John?"

"No." Mathew shook his head slowly. "The drinking was to block it all out. The accident, the fact that you weren't speaking to me, and yes, the ghost who was trying to eject me from my own body. I had some free will, but when John got nasty, he also got strong, and I wasn't able to do anything to stop him."

"If he's the one behind the lawsuit, then you can pick up the phone and call it off," Austin said. "You wouldn't have a problem with that, would you?"

"No." His father hung his head and let out a deep sigh as he pulled his phone out and tapped on a number. It wasn't long before he was instructing his lawyer to drop the suit. When he ended the call, he looked up. "It's done. And I'm fine with it. It's what you wanted," he said to Peggy. "I just don't understand how or why you'd leave a stranger so much money. It's... unusual to say the least."

Peggy eyed him suspiciously. "I thought now that you're dropping the suit, you'd drop the act, too."

"What act?" Mathew and Austin said at the same time.

She narrowed her eyes at her son. "The act that you don't know who Gideon is. For the life of me, I never understood why you pretended you didn't have another son. Or that

Austin had a brother."

Both men went still and stared wide-eyed at Peggy. Then Austin turned to glare at his father. "Gideon is your son?"

"I…" Mathew shook his head. "How is that possible? I only have one son. Austin."

"Does Sheila Sheraton ring any bells?" Peggy asked.

Mathew gasped. "Throm's wife? The Gideon who moved to Keating Hollow is Throm and Sheila's boy?"

"Not Throm and Sheila's. *Yours* and Sheila's," Peggy said, placing her hands on her hips. "Did it never occur to you that Gideon might be yours?"

Mathew shook his head. "No. I didn't even know they had a son until he was grown and making news for himself. Why didn't Sheila tell me?"

"Throm," Peggy said. "She chose Throm. After you broke off the affair, she went back to him. And because you never went after her, I never got to know my grandson until he moved here to Keating Hollow a short while ago." She shook her head, her disappointment radiating off her like a beacon.

"How did you find out?" Austin asked her. "How did you know Gideon is my brother?"

"Oh, that's easy. It's his eyes. The moment I saw them, I knew those were Steele eyes. Then I did the background on him, got his birthdate, and realized he was born eight months after your father sent Sheila away. But I still managed to snag his DNA and had a paternity test done. I was going to confront Mathew about it, but my heart gave out before I could chew him out for being so selfish."

"I didn't know, Mom," Mathew said. "I swear I didn't. When Sheila left, that was that. I didn't see her again, and I knew nothing of her life with Throm. He knew about the affair, and after that, he never spoke to me again. I can't say I blame him either."

Austin stood and turned to his father. "Do something about the issue at Hollow Books. Do it today." When he glanced at his grandmother, her form had already gone translucent. "And you, no more secrets."

"I was waiting for him to tell you himself. I never dreamed he didn't know." She kissed her palm and blew Austin a kiss. "Now that you've been filled in, get to know Gideon. He's a great guy."

Austin nodded. "He is. And I will."

"Good. Now, I have somewhere to be," she said and waved as she faded away into the ether.

"She didn't go into the light," Brinn said, looking thoughtful. "I wonder where she went?"

"You're probably the only one who can answer that," Wanda teased. "Want to call her back?"

"Not on your life. Peggy Steele is a badass. I don't want her kicking mine," Brinn said.

Austin strode over to her, kissed the top of her head, and said, "Let's go home. I'm exhausted."

"I thought you'd never ask." She slipped her arm through his and waited for him to guide her out the front door.

He glanced back at his father. "After you clear up the mess with the bookstore, you can stop by the house. Maybe then we can try to form some sort of relationship."

His father nodded solemnly. "I'd like that very much."

Austin just nodded. He wasn't a fool. He knew a lot of the things his father had done over the years hadn't been due to the ghost. He wasn't going to let Mathew Steele blame every shitty thing he'd done on the fact that he'd had a parasite ghost. The behaviors were repeated offenses that had spanned more than just one decade. But Austin was willing to give it a try. He had to just for his own peace of mind.

And maybe for his heart, too. No one wanted to imagine that their parent was a selfish asshole. Maybe, just maybe, this would be Mathew Steele's second chance.

Wanda waved from her SUV as Austin helped Brinn into his car. They both looked over at the front porch where Austin's dad was standing to see them off.

Once again, Austin noted just how broken he looked. He hoped for his father's sake that after a few good nights' sleep that he'd start to look more himself again. But Austin supposed he'd look like hell if a ghost had taken over his body, too.

Only time would tell with his recovery.

"Ready to go home, love?" Austin asked Brinn.

She nodded. "More than ready. I can't wait to snuggle up in our bed with Dru and Oz and the feline gang."

"Me, too." He grinned at her, elated that she was thinking of his bed as theirs. The truth was, he'd give her anything she wanted as long as it made her happy. Even if it meant getting a new bed. Or three more dogs. If she wanted it, he wanted to give it to her.

"Why are you looking at me like that?" she asked.

"Just brainstorming some ideas for what we're going to do in that bed when we get home. That's all."

She beamed. "Drive faster."

IN THE DAYS that followed the showdown at Mathew's house, the problems at the bookstore did indeed go away and the shelves were stocked again. The lawsuit was dismissed. Austin and Mathew had been working on trying to rebuild their relationship now that his father was no longer possessed. It wasn't everything Austin hoped for, but they were making progress. They weren't really close, but they had formed a mutual respect for each other.

Austin had purchased the old radio station building that had been retrofitted with a recording studio not that long ago, so he didn't have to do as much traveling back and forth from LA for his business. Levi, Seth, and Logan had outfitted it, but now that Levi and Seth were out touring, they didn't need it anymore. He and Brinn had started welding classes and had become quite the amateur pastry chefs. There were still a lot of things on her bucket list, but they were taking their time, enjoying each one.

And Gideon was spending a lot more time over at Austin's house. It had been weird for both of them to embrace the brother label, but Gideon had confessed it was a relief.

Gideon had confided that he'd already known his father wasn't his biological father, but he'd never known who was. All he'd known was that his mother had slept with his dad's best friend and they'd had a falling out. But since it had all happened so many years before Gideon discovered he wasn't Throm's biological son, he hadn't ever been able to discover who it was, and Throm wouldn't tell him. Now that Gideon knew it was Mathew, they were making an effort to get to know each other. Surprisingly, it was going a lot smoother than Austin's journey with his father. Probably because they didn't have all the baggage and history that Austin and Mathew did.

"You're a good brother," Gideon said one evening while holding a beer in one hand and scribbling on a note pad with the other.

"I am? Why?" Austin asked him.

"Because you always let me win at poker," he said, chuckling.

Austin shook his head. "*Let* might be overstating things."

Gideon snorted. "I was just giving you the benefit of the doubt."

"Okay. That's enough," Miranda said, striding into the room holding a chicken canister. "The cookies are gone, Austin. I thought you said they were in this. Looks like your chicken ate them all."

Brinn giggled. "I love those canisters. But it does make it hard to tell when the cookies are gone." She got up, took the canister, and said, "Come on, I know where there might be another stash."

It didn't take long for the women to return, and this time each of them was holding a sugar cookie and laughing at something one of them had said.

Miranda walked over to Gideon and placed a hand on his shoulder. "Come on. We've been here long enough. Let's let these two lovebirds have their evening back."

Gideon glanced at Austin and immediately stood. "Okay. On it. Take me home, woman."

Miranda rolled her eyes. "Call me woman again, and I'll swat you on the nose. It's Miranda. Remember?"

"Of course I do." His eyes were glassy and his smile a little sloppy.

"How much have you two had to drink?" she asked.

"Not much. Only…" He counted off on his fingers, scowled, and then said, "I have no idea."

Brinn burst out laughing.

Austin laughed, too, and for the first time, he felt that his life was perfect. *Almost* perfect. There was one thing left to do.

"Austin made me do it," Gideon said.

"No, I didn't. I stopped after two beers." Austin raised his eyebrow at the more than half-dozen empty beer bottles on the table.

"Pretty sure Miranda and Brinn helped," Gideon said.

"We weren't that much help," Brinn said, grinning at him. It wasn't often they saw Gideon drunk. She found it amusing.

"Let's go," Miranda said, pulling him toward the front door. "Time to get you home, get some water in you, and put you to bed." She glanced at Brinn and Austin. "See you next Friday. I can't wait to get to Napa and ride that balloon."

"Same," Brinn said. They'd decided to invite Miranda and Gideon on their trip after Miranda had said a balloon ride was also on her bucket list.

Gideon wrapped his arm around her and whispered something in her ear that made her giggle.

Brinn grinned while Austin said something about meeting up the next day to work on the art and music program. Gideon raised his hand, acknowledging he'd heard him, and then the pair walked out, leaving Austin and Brinn alone.

Austin turned to Brinn. "Will you take a walk with me?"

"Now?" She stared at him as if he'd lost his mind. "It's almost midnight. Are you sure you didn't have more than two beers?"

He chuckled. "I'm sure. It's just a walk around the property. Say yes. I have a surprise for you."

She eyed him suspiciously but said, "Okay. You know how I like surprises."

"I do." Grinning, he took her hand and led her out of the back door and down the freshly cleared path that led to the far corner of the property. In the days after the exorcism of his father, he'd spent a lot of time outdoors, working to improve his grandmother's property. One of the things he'd done was clear a path to his favorite spot.

When they reached the clearing, Brinn let out a surprised gasp. "You did this?"

He nodded. They were at the tree that had the initials carved in the trunk. It had turned out to be a favorite spot for both of them, so Austin had gotten a wrought iron bench and a couple of matching chairs, turning it into an outdoor seating area. "Take a seat," he said.

She did as he asked and leaned back, staring up at the stars through the small clearing. "It's gorgeous."

"So are you."

She smiled at him and then glanced over at the tree with the initials. "Did you ever figure out who those initials belong to?"

"I did. My father, of all people, knew." He took her hand in both of his as he continued. "They stand for Margaret Carlisle and Bud Davis."

"Isn't Margaret your grandmother's name?" she asked.

"Yes, and Carlisle is her maiden name."

She frowned. "But who is Bud Davis?"

"He was her first husband."

Brinn's eyes widened. "She was married before she married your grandfather?"

"I know. It was a surprise to me, too," he said softly. "He died just six months after they were married. It was a tragic accident, and my dad said he thinks she never really got over it. He said she used to come out here a lot when she needed time to herself."

"But your grandfather, they had a good marriage, right?" Brinn asked.

He nodded. His grandfather had been a fierce businessman,

but he was loved by the community due to his generosity. He was sure his grandmother had loved him. But that didn't mean she didn't grieve for her first love. Even if Austin had moved on to someone else other than Brinn, he'd have always held a special place in his heart for her. "They did. But you know how it is. One never gets over their first love."

She reached up and pressed her palm to his cheek. "No. They don't."

Austin slid off the bench down onto one knee and looked up at her. "Do you know what today is?"

"Tuesday?" she asked, her voice shaking a little even as she smiled down at him.

"It's the anniversary of our very first kiss."

Tears shone in those brilliant eyes of hers as her smile widened. "You remember the day."

"Of course I do." He pulled out a small ring box. "I remember everything. I've always wanted you, Brinn. I can't remember a day when I didn't want you with me, in my life, by my side. I love you. I've always loved you. Will you—"

"Yes!" she cried before he could get the words out. "Yes. A million times, yes."

He laughed as he blinked back his own tears and then slid the ring onto her finger.

She pulled him back up to the bench and pressed both palms to his cheeks. "I love you, too, Austin Steele."

Austin leaned in and kissed his fiancée. They sat there for a long time, kissing, whispering, and holding each other. And just when they were ready to walk back to the house, two figures appeared right by the tree.

"Look," Brinn whispered, pointing to them.

The two ghosts were young, in their early twenties, and they were holding hands as they stared at Brinn and Austin.

Then the young woman smiled, and Austin's heart started to beat faster. It was his grandmother, Peggy. But the man who she was with was not his grandfather.

"It's time to go, Bud," she said softly. "Our work here is done."

He glanced down at her, touched his hand to the carved initials, and nodded.

Peggy smiled softly at Austin and Brinn. "Be good to each other, and treasure every day that you have."

Austin nodded. "We will."

The pair turned and walked through the woods toward a faint white light. And as they stepped into it, Austin knew that was the last time he'd ever see his grandmother.

Brinn sniffed softly beside him. "That was beautiful."

He nodded as he glanced down at her, tightened his hold, and said, "Let's go home."

CHAPTER 26

*Z*ya took a long sip of her hard cider, wishing she'd decided to stay in for Valentine's day. She'd been in Keating Hollow for a little over a year now, and still sometimes felt like an outsider. But that was probably because unless Brinn coaxed her out, she was a bit of a recluse. And after putting Brinn off for the past month, she'd finally caved and agreed to venture out for a couple of drinks.

The party was being held at the Townsend Brewery, and the best thing she could say about it was that the booze was excellent. She had no idea why she'd agreed to go. The place was full of couples, each of them staring at each other with hearts in their eyes.

Wasn't that one of the reasons she'd left Salem? To get away from love? Or more specifically, from the man she'd thought she'd been in love with only to find out he was in love with three other people.

"Zya!" Brinn called as she spotted her. "Hey, you made it."

The pair had been spending a lot of time together recently. Zya had been teaching Brinn how to put her guards up so she wasn't overrun with ghosts all the time. And Brinn had been a good friend, pulling Zya into the Keating Hollow fold. She'd dragged her to multiple weddings during the previous summer. All of them were lovely and magical and had pulled at Zya's mostly hardened heartstrings. Zya found that she genuinely liked Brinn and her friends, though she was still having trouble opening up about her past. But who could blame her? After everything that went down in Salem, she was ready for a fresh start.

"Hey, Brinn. Where's your other half?"

She gestured to a group of men on the other side of the pub. "Over there, trying to form a group to challenge us ladies to a golf cart race."

Zya grinned and shook her head. "You guys and your races. I thought you were giving them a break after the last fiasco. Didn't Wanda's cart end up with two flat tires, and wasn't there something about needing an engine replacement?"

Brinn grimaced. "Yeah. That was bad. But Abby and I finally beat Wanda, and Abby didn't lose that awful bet. Now I get to use Abby's cart anytime I want. Though don't tell Wanda. She's still smarting from that epic beatdown."

Chuckling, Zya shook her head. She'd never known people like the women of Keating Hollow. They had the kinds of friendships that Zya had always envied and never been able to cultivate for herself before. But now... maybe she could be a part of it too. If she stayed long enough.

Zya had a habit of picking up and leaving. It was her fatal flaw. This time, however, she'd opened a shop, praying it was the incentive to keep her in one place. Keating Hollow just made her feel like maybe this time she'd found home.

"So can I count on you for the golf cart race?" Brinn asked her. "After the party of course."

"Sure," she said, unable to resist being included.

The door swung open and a tall, gorgeous woman with auburn colored hair walked in. She was beaming as she waved her phone in the air. "It happened!" she cried. "Silas has finally been nominated for an Oscar!"

Everyone in the brewery cheered and congratulated Shannon. Silas was her brother, and she managed his acting career. Everyone in the pub chattered about Silas and asked about his boyfriend Levi, who was out doing his own thing, making a name for himself in the music industry. It sounded like they were both living charmed lives, and Zya wondered how that would work out for them. She'd had long-distance relationships before, but they never worked out. Someone always cheated.

It wasn't long before Brinn was pulling Zya outside to include her in the golf cart shenanigans, but just as she was getting ready to climb in, her phone vibrated with a text alert.

She glanced down at her phone and did a doubletake.

Brody was texting her. Her Brody. The Brody she hadn't seen for five years.

She read the text. *I'm at your house.*

Zya frowned. *In Salem?*

No. In Keating Hollow.

That was impossible. Zya stared down at the phone, her heart nearly beating out of her chest.

"Zya? Are you okay?" Brinn asked.

She glanced up at her friend. "I... I have to go. Sorry, Brinn. Can I get a raincheck?"

"Sure. But what's wrong?"

"Nothing. I..." She felt her lips curve into a smile. "My best friend just surprised me and is at my house. I have to go."

Without waiting for Brinn to respond, Zya texted back. *I'll be right there.*

With her heart racing and her palms sweating, Zya hurried home. She couldn't believe Brody was there. She'd been half in love with him since the moment he'd punched her first boyfriend for breaking up with her on her birthday. They'd been best friends ever since.

Well, they had been until he'd moved to Europe to be with his French girlfriend.

But now he was back. In Keating Hollow. And he'd come to see her.

She spotted him the moment she pulled to a stop at her house in the woods. He was sitting on her porch swing, his head in his hands, looking defeated.

Zya exited the car and called, "Brody?"

He jerked his head up and stood. That's when she noticed the little girl standing next to him.

She frowned as she walked up onto her porch. They stood there staring at each other for a minute, until Brody finally said, "Zya, I'd like you to meet my daughter, Winnie."

Zya blinked. *Daughter?* Had he just said daughter? Brody had a kid and hadn't told her? Her world tilted, and she felt like she'd been pulled under water, unable to breathe. Finally, she got a hold of herself and kneeled down in front of the gorgeous girl with thick black curls. "Hi, Winnie. I'm Zya."

"Hi," she said shyly with the sweetest smile Zya had ever seen.

Her heart melted into a puddle of goo. But when she looked back up at Brody, she narrowed her eyes and mouthed, *Daughter?*

Brody took her hand and pulled her to him, giving her the hug she'd needed. But she was having some sort of out-of-body experience because he had a daughter and she hadn't known. Then he whispered in her ear, "I'm all she has left. Can we stay?"

Zya pulled back from him, saw there was trauma lurking in his eyes, and nodded. She had no idea what had happened or why Brody had kept it from her, but he was here now. And no matter how much she wanted to yell and scream at him for keeping her in the dark, she couldn't. Her heart wouldn't let her.

Silently, she moved to the door, opened it, and waved them in.

DEANNA'S BOOK LIST

Witches of Keating Hollow:
Soul of the Witch
Heart of the Witch
Spirit of the Witch
Dreams of the Witch
Courage of the Witch
Love of the Witch
Power of the Witch
Essence of the Witch
Muse of the Witch
Vision of the Witch
Waking of the Witch
Honor of the Witch
Promise of the Witch

Witches of Christmas Grove:
A Witch For Mr. Holiday
A Witch For Mr. Christmas
A Witch For Mr. Winter

A Witch For Mr. Mistletoe

Premonition Pointe Novels:
Witching For Grace
Witching For Hope
Witching For Joy
Witching For Clarity
Witching For Moxie
Witching For Kismet

Miss Matched Midlife Dating Agency:
Star-crossed Witch
Honor-bound Witch
Outmatched Witch

Jade Calhoun Novels:
Haunted on Bourbon Street
Witches of Bourbon Street
Demons of Bourbon Street
Angels of Bourbon Street
Shadows of Bourbon Street
Incubus of Bourbon Street
Bewitched on Bourbon Street
Hexed on Bourbon Street
Dragons of Bourbon Street

Pyper Rayne Novels:
Spirits, Stilettos, and a Silver Bustier
Spirits, Rock Stars, and a Midnight Chocolate Bar
Spirits, Beignets, and a Bayou Biker Gang
Spirits, Diamonds, and a Drive-thru Daiquiri Stand
Spirits, Spells, and Wedding Bells

Ida May Chronicles:
Witched To Death
Witch, Please
Stop Your Witchin'

Crescent City Fae Novels:
Influential Magic
Irresistible Magic
Intoxicating Magic

Last Witch Standing:
Bewitched by Moonlight
Soulless at Sunset
Bloodlust By Midnight
Bitten At Daybreak

Witch Island Brides:
The Wolf's New Year Bride
The Vampire's Last Dance
The Warlock's Enchanted Kiss
The Shifter's First Bite

Destiny Novels:
Defining Destiny
Accepting Fate

Wolves of the Rising Sun:
Jace
Aiden
Luc
Craved
Silas

Darien

Wren

Black Bear Outlaws:

Cyrus

Chase

Cole

Bayou Springs Alien Mail Order Brides:

Zeke

Gunn

Echo

ABOUT THE AUTHOR

New York Times and USA Today bestselling author, Deanna Chase, is a native Californian, transplanted to the slower paced lifestyle of southeastern Louisiana. When she isn't writing, she is often goofing off with her husband in New Orleans or playing with her two shih tzu dogs. For more information and updates on newest releases visit her website at deannachase.com.

www.ingramcontent.com/pod-product-compliance
Lightning Source LLC
Chambersburg PA
CBHW020056180626
46812CB00006B/2345